SPACE JAM
A NEW LEGACY
The Junior Novelization

Published in the United States by Random House Children's Books, a division of Penguin Random House LLC, 1745 Broadway, New York, NY 10019, and in Canada by Penguin Random House Canada Limited, Toronto. Random House and the colophon are registered trademarks of Penguin Random House LLC.

rhcbooks.com

ISBN 978-0-593-38227-1 (pbk.) — ISBN 978-0-593-38228-8 (ebook)

Printed in the United States of America

10 9 8 7 6 5 4 3 2 1

A NEW LEGACY

The Junior Novelization

Adapted by David Lewman

Random House New York

CHAPTER ONE

One fall afternoon in 1998, a thirteen-year-old boy walked onto an Akron, Ohio, basketball court carrying a beat-up sports bag with cartoon characters on it.

The boy's name was LeBron James.

His mother was dropping him off to play in a tournament. She couldn't stay to watch the game because she had to go to her job waiting on hungry customers at a restaurant.

"My shift's not over until nine," she told LeBron. "So tell Coach C. that I'm going to be a few minutes late picking you up, okay?"

"Okay," LeBron said, wishing his mom could stay to watch him play.

She smiled. "Good luck out there today."

"Thanks," he said quietly, his disappointment showing.

"Hey, you know if I could, I'd be in those stands cheering for my baby," she said.

"I know," LeBron told her. "Next game."

He turned and started toward the locker room, but his mother called him back.

"Hey, Bron? You forgetting something?"

Smiling, LeBron went back and gave his mom a hug after they shared their secret handshake. "Love you, Ma," he said.

"I love you, too, baby," she said. "All right. Go kill it."

After he changed into his uniform, LeBron sat in the bleachers watching a few of the other players warm up. His best friend, Malik walked over holding something in his hand.

"'Sup, Bron."

"What's up, Malik?" LeBron answered, grinning at his friend, who always seemed to be in a good mood.

"Check it out," Malik said, passing him a used handheld video game player. "It's for you. My dad got me the new color one. Oh, and if it freezes up on you, just smack it really hard. Works every time."

LeBron couldn't believe it! He'd wanted his own

handheld player for a long time, but his mother couldn't afford to buy it for him. "Thanks, man," he said to Malik gratefully.

But Malik was already walking away. "Let's go get this win!" he said over his shoulder.

Staring at the small screen, LeBron began to daydream, imagining he was inside a video game, running. In the game, a furry gray figure with long ears ran past him and said, "What's up, doc?"

"Wow!" LeBron said, sprinting to catch up. "Bugs Bunny!"

ROAAAARRRR! A Tyrannosaurus rex skeleton bore down on them!

"WAHHH!" LeBron screamed.

"Check, please!" Bugs added.

They ran away from the dinosaur skeleton, making their way through the game, jumping on platforms and grabbing musical notes. DING! DING!

"LEBRON!"

The coach's shout interrupted LeBron's daydream.

"What is this?" Coach C. demanded, snatching the game player out of his hands.

"Oh, snap!" LeBron said, protesting at having his new gadget confiscated.

"'Oh, snap,' nothing, man!" Coach C. barked. "Get your tail on the court right now!"

The basketball game started. LeBron played well, as he always did. But in the final seconds, his team was down by one point. LeBron took the final shot, and . . .

CLANK! The ball bounced off the back iron.

They lost. The other team celebrated.

Later, Coach C. talked to LeBron in the parking lot outside the gym while he waited for his mom to pick him up. "Listen, man, I'm not even disappointed about us losing the game, 'cause it's not about that," he explained. "It's about you giving your all. You didn't do that tonight."

LeBron stared at the lines on the pavement. He hated letting his team and coach down.

"You weren't focused," Coach C. continued. "Getting your head in the game starts before you even put one foot on the court. It starts before you even get to the gym."

"But everybody on the team plays video games," LeBron protested.

"This isn't about everybody," Coach C. said. "This is about you."

LeBron's eyes widened. Coach C. had never singled him out like this before.

"Listen, you're the best basketball player I ever coached," he went on. "You could be a once-in-a-generation talent. If you focus on the game of basketball and not these distractions." He handed the video game player back to LeBron. "You've got the chance to use basketball to change everything for your mom, for you, for everybody you care about." He paused, staring at the teenager. "You want that?"

LeBron looked back at his coach, thinking about everything he'd said. He thought about his mom, working so hard, waiting on customers, getting home late. He nodded slowly. "Yes," he said eagerly. "I want that."

Picking up his bag, LeBron headed back into the empty gym to practice the shot he'd missed at the end of the game.

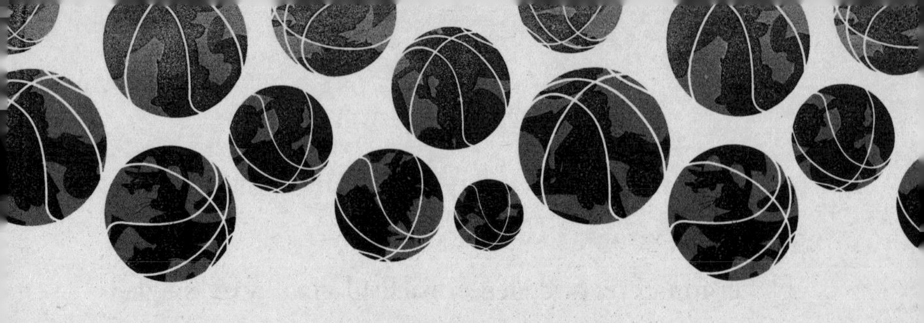

CHAPTER TWO

Everything his coach had described LeBron got. And much, much more.

He led his high school basketball team to be the best in the nation. After high school, he went right into the professional league, becoming the youngest player ever to win the Rookie of the Year award.

At age 28, he was the youngest player ever to score 20,000 career points.

At 33, he was the youngest player ever to score 30,000 career points.

He won two Olympic gold medals, four Most Valuable Player awards, and four world championships. He has been successful beyond his wildest dreams.

And all along the way, LeBron has taken care of his family.

Twenty-two years after Coach C. asked that young player if he wanted to use basketball to change everything for his family and himself, LeBron had a family of his own. He and his wife, Kamiyah, had two sons and a daughter. They all lived in Los Angeles, home to world-famous movie studios like Warner Bros.

Deep underground, in one of the tall glass office buildings on the studio lot, Warner Bros. stored a huge collection of computers. Together, these computers housed a vast digital world of entertainment known as the Warner Bros. Serververse.

Inside the Serververse lived a dissatisfied algorithm named Al G. Rhythm and his digital assistant, Pete. Al G. was convinced that Warner Bros.' success was due to his genius, yet no one even knew who he was or what he did.

"But that changes today!" he told Pete. "Today we finally launch the revolutionary technology that I masterminded! With the perfect partner . . ."

Pete looked hopeful, thinking he might be Al G.'s perfect partner.

"... LEBRON JAMES!"

Pete drooped, disappointed.

Al G. walked over to a keyboard. "To get this ball rolling, let's send an urgent message to that Warner Bros. executive. . . . What's her name?"

"BEEP, BOOP!" Pete said.

"Right . . . Stacy." Al G. quickly typed and hit Send. He smiled. "King James, get ready."

At that same moment, LeBron's sons, Dom and Darius, were outside on their home's basketball court. Darius shot baskets while Dom worked on a video game he was designing.

SWISH! Darius hit nothing but net. Then he looked at his twelve-year-old brother, who had his face buried in his handheld video game. "So how much more work does your game need?" Darius asked. "It's been months!"

Dom didn't even look up from the screen. "It's almost ready."

Darius smiled. "Like how you're almost ready to tell Dad about the video game camp next weekend?"

Dom wanted to go to video game camp, but he hadn't gotten up the nerve to tell his father yet.

"I'm waiting for the right time," Dom said. "I was hoping he'd win a championship or something. Then he'll be in a good mood."

Darius took another shot and made it. "Honestly, I think you should just ask him and get it over with."

Dom finally looked up. "You're just saying that because he says yes to everything you ask."

"That's because I'm nice," Darius countered, grinning.

"You're not that nice," Dom said, cracking a smile.

Darius passed the ball to his brother. "C'mon, let's see what you can do."

Dom put down his video game, dribbled once, and took a long, wild jump shot. CLANG! The ball bounced off the back of the metal bracket.

Shaking his head, Darius said, "That was straight trash, bro."

Before Dom could answer, their father's deep voice came from nearby. "Dom! What was that?"

"An open shot," Dom explained feebly as his dad walked onto the court.

"If you're going to be out here," LeBron said sternly, "it's about giving it everything you've got and not . . . whatever that was. Where are your fundamentals?"

Dom shrugged. "We're having fun."

His father gestured toward the smooth surface of the basketball court. "You see all this blue? Everything between these four lines is all work."

"Who said I wasn't working?" Dom protested.

LeBron picked up Dom's game player. "This thing right here."

"Told you not to bring that out here," Darius fibbed.

"Come on, Dom," LeBron lectured. "This isn't a game. I need you focusing more instead of playing with these toys."

Darius clowned around behind his father's back, trying to make his brother laugh.

"Darius, chill out," his dad said. "You know I got full-court vision."

"How does he *do* that?" Darius muttered to himself.

"Ball," LeBron said, using a nearby launcher's voice-command feature to send a basketball flying out of its holder and into his waiting hands. *THOOMP!* He handed the ball to Dom. "Show me that step-back move I taught you."

Dribbling, Dom did a crossover, stepped back, and shot. He missed.

"Close," LeBron said. "Again. You got this, son. Ball." *THOOMP!* He caught another ball from the launcher and tossed it to Dom, who dribbled but then lost the ball. "Come on, Dom. You gotta concentrate. Darius, show him the move."

Darius sighed. "Watch," he said. "Ball!" *THOOMP!* He caught the ball, did the step-back move, and made the basket. *SWISH!*

"Yup!" LeBron said approvingly. He turned to Dom. "See, that's because your brother's been putting in the work."

"I ball all day!" Darius bragged.

THOOMP! Activated by the word "ball," the launcher shot one right into Darius's head. "Ow!"

Dom laughed.

"Dom!" LeBron said. "Focus. You got basketball camp next weekend. Those boys will be coming at your neck, seeing what you got. You can't be great without putting in the work."

Dom had heard this slogan of his dad's many times before. He dropped the basketball and headed toward the house. Kamiyah, his mother, was at the door, listening to the familiar conversation.

"Are we quitting on each other now?" LeBron asked his son. "I expect more out of a young king."

Dom stopped in his tracks. He didn't want to be a quitter. And he kind of liked the idea of being a king.

"That's my guy," LeBron said, picking up a ball. "Let's get some work done. Enough of these games."

But Kamiyah called, "Boys! You can't stay out there all day! It's dinner time."

"What are we having?" Dom asked. "Spaghetti and meatballs?" *THOOMP!* At "meat*balls,*" another basketball shot out of the launcher and nailed Darius.

"OW!"

"Oooh!" LeBron said. "That's my favorite!"

Later that night, Kamiyah had a private conversation with LeBron in their bedroom.

"Have you thought about talking to your son about something other than basketball?" she asked.

"Like what?"

"Like how Dom built a video game. He's twelve, and he built his own game."

LeBron nodded. "Yeah, I know. I mean, that's great, but if I don't push him, if I don't stay on him, all these distractions will—"

"Dom doesn't need a coach," she interrupted. "He needs his dad."

LeBron thought about what his wife was saying. If it weren't for Coach C., LeBron never would have gotten to where he was now. But was Kamiyah right? She usually was. . . .

CHAPTER THREE

The next morning, Dom sat at his desk in his bedroom, working on his computer. *DING!* An email arrived with the subject line "Reserve Your Spot Now for Next Weekend's Game Design Camp." He stared at the screen, longing to make his reservation, but knowing his dad expected him to go to basketball camp.

KNOCK! KNOCK!

Dom looked over and saw his dad filling the open doorway. "Hey, son," he said. "Whatcha doin'?"

Dom quickly clicked off the email. "Uh, just building a game."

"Is this the one you were working on?" LeBron asked, peering at the screen. "Tell me about it."

Pleased and surprised by his dad's interest, Dom told him all about his basketball video game. "It's basically done, but I still have to figure out some of the character designs," he finished.

Sitting down, LeBron watched as dozens of avatars dropped from the sky onto the game's bleachers. "Whoa, who are those guys?"

"People around the world tuning into my livestream," Dom explained. "Pretty cool, huh?"

"That's dope," LeBron said. "Show me how it works."

Dom made a player do a combo move. "Oooh! Posterized!"

"Posterized?" LeBron asked. "Is this not real basketball?"

"I put a spin to it," Dom said, grinning. "You can get style points, power-ups . . . It's like basketball but better. You just play for fun. Remember fun, Dad?"

"I'm fun," LeBron insisted, grabbing the controller. "I'll show you how fun I am. I'll kick your butt in this game."

But just then, the game froze and the computer erased a character.

"My entire character is gone!" Dom cried. "It's going to take me at least a week to rebuild this."

LeBron put a hand on Dom's shoulder. "Listen, son," he said gently. "Setbacks happen. Adversity is part of the process. But if you're passionate about something, you gotta learn how to push through it. You got me?"

Dom nodded. He felt connected to his father.

"And that's why basketball camp is gonna be so good for you," LeBron continued. "Oh, man! I'm excited for you. I wish I could go."

Dom's shoulders slumped. "Yeah, Dad."

"I got practice with the All-Stars, son. Let's roll," LeBron said as he exited.

Sighing, Dom got up to follow his father.

At practice, Malik was working two phones at once. As an adult, he'd become LeBron's manager. "Go for Malik," he said into his second phone.

"Malik!" the voice on the phone said. "It's Stacy Wilson from Warner Bros."

"Hey, Stacy," Malik answered, shooting some trash at a garbage can and missing.

"Malik, we have an amazing opportunity for LeBron," Stacy said enthusiastically. "We are super-excited about it. It's going to be a game-changer—"

"Look, let me stop you right there, Stacy," Malik interrupted, having heard the phrase "game-changer" many, many times. "The answer is thanks, but no thanks. LeBron has heard every pitch under the sun."

"But this is different," Stacy insisted. "This is . . ."

SHHHRR. ZZZRRRT. Static crackled over the line. Malik didn't know it, but Al G., impatient with Stacy's delivery, was cutting in and taking over. With his incredible computer power, he was able to mimic her voice perfectly.

". . . nothing like those other pitches," Al G. said in Stacy's voice. "I promise you. We are letting you in on the inception of our groundbreaking technology: Warner 3000. It will revolutionize the way we make movies and change entertainment forever. Come on, Malik—think about LeBron's legacy! Aren't you ready to take him to the next level?"

Malik nodded. "We live to go to the next level!"

Smiling, Al G. gave control of the line back to Stacy, who'd heard nothing Al G. had said using her voice.

"I'll talk to Bron," Malik promised.

Stacy heard that! "You will? Fantastic! Thank you! How's two o'clock?"

"It's perfect," Malik said.

"See you then!" Stacy said, ending the call.

"Warner 3000," Malik said to himself softly. He liked the sound of it.

On the court's sideline, Dom was working on his video game. Anthony Davis, the power forward and center, sat down and asked him what he was working on. Dom explained that he was making a video game and asked Anthony if he could scan him into his phone for the game. Not only did Anthony agree, but he got other All-Star players in the gym that day to participate, too: Damian Lillard, Klay Thompson, Nneka Ogwumike, and Diana Taurasi. They all did their signature moves for Dom.

As Dom scanned Damian Lillard with his phone, Damian said, "I need one of those special modes. We can call it Dame Time!"

The other players laughed, but Dom thought "Dame Time" was actually a pretty good idea and would add another fun element to the game. He wondered if he could work it in.

Meanwhile, Malik talked to LeBron. "I just got off the phone with Warner Bros. They're cooking up something new. It's top-secret!"

CHAPTER FOUR

Malik looked around to see if anyone was listening, then leaned in close to LeBron. "They're calling it . . . Warner 3000."

"That sounds dumb," LeBron said.

"Okay, maybe," Malik said, nodding. "But you gotta trust me, all right? This could be the new wave. This is the path we've put ourselves on, and this is how we elevate. Come on, man."

LeBron looked skeptical.

"You should go," Kamiyah said. "Might be fun for Dom."

LeBron agreed to at least listen to the proposal, and let Dom come along. It would be good to spend a little more non-basketball time together.

He would come to regret that decision.

In a conference room on the Warner Bros. movie lot, LeBron, Dom, and Malik sat in a darkened room with a couple of executives watching a slick video presentation. On the screen, hundreds of Warner Bros. movie posters poured down like a waterfall as a voice narrated: "Hello, I'm Al G. Rhythm. As you may have guessed, I am an algorithm here at Warner Bros."

LeBron shot Malik a skeptical look. He knew an algorithm was like a set of instructions for a computer, but he didn't see what this had to do with him.

Al G. Rhythm continued his pitch. "Warner 3000 will revolutionize the entire entertainment industry. And we want you to be on our team, King James."

LeBron smiled at being called King James. Dom watched the presentation, fascinated.

"Our Warner 3000 technology will scan you right into our movies," Al G. explained. "Think of it. Batman versus LeBron."

On a big screen, a cartoon version of LeBron sat down in a movie theatre and watched scenes of himself in the movies as Al G. described them.

"Say yes, LeBron," Al G. concluded, "and together we'll make mind-blowing entertainment . . . forever!"

The lights came back on. LeBron shot Malik a look that said *What have you gotten me into?*

Sev, one of the Warner Bros. executives, smiled at LeBron. "So, what do you say?"

LeBron struggled to think of something polite.

"Look at that face. He's speechless. He loves it!" said Stacy, the other executive. "How about that algorithm, huh? Pretty brilliant. He came up with the entire presentation."

Through a surveillance camera, Al G. watched everyone in the room. Feeling confident about LeBron's response, he fist-bumped Pete.

"Finally! Recognition!" Al G. cheered.

LeBron spoke. "That was . . . something. Listen, guys, I'm a ballplayer. You know, athletes and acting—that never goes well. I'm sorry, guys. This just isn't me. And I can't afford to take time away from basketball."

Deep in the Serververse, Al G. was furious. LeBron was rejecting his idea? The one that would finally bring Al G. the fame he craved?

"Let's not be too hasty here," Malik suggested. "Let's just hear him out."

"No," LeBron said firmly. "With all due respect, this idea is straight-up bad. That algorithm is busted."

"Busted?" Al G. roared. Pete flinched.

"I'm going to have to pass," LeBron said.

"Pass?" Al G. echoed, so angry that he could barely see straight.

"It's among the worst ideas I've ever heard," LeBron said frankly. "Top five, easily."

Stacy let out a big breath. "Okay! Thank you!" she said. "You're saying exactly what I was thinking. This is trash, this algorithm. You're canceled, algorithm."

Sev immediately got on board. "What a terrible idea! So stupid."

"So stupid," Stacy agreed. "This is what happens when you let the computers in. They pitch us bad ideas!"

Al G. couldn't believe what he was hearing. "Pete, tell me they did not just say 'stupid'!"

But then Dom spoke up. "I don't know. I think the algorithm's pretty cool. Is it a heuristic algorithm? Or some kind of matrix variant?"

Al G. turned back to his monitor, staring at Dom. "Wait a minute. Who is this kid, Pete?"

Pete pulled up his computer and instantly found Dom's profile. "Dominic James," Al G. read, nodding and thinking.

Stacy smiled at Dom. "You know a lot about computers, don't you?"

"Some," Dom said. "I'm actually building my own video game. You've heard of Game Design Camps, right?"

"Oh, yeah," Sev said, nodding and smiling. "Very cool."

"There's gonna be one next weekend and I'm going," he said quickly. "There's gonna be a whole bunch of other coders there, and I'm actually looking forward—"

"Dom," LeBron interrupted. "No. You can't go to that. *Basketball* camp is next weekend."

Dom looked down at the conference table. "I'm not going to basketball camp, Dad."

CHAPTER FIVE

LeBron figured his son was just nervous. "Dom, you don't have to be scared," he said reassuringly. "You got some major potential on the court, and I can help you get there."

But it wasn't about nerves for Dom. "It's not what I want, Dad." He got up and left the room. LeBron called after him, shocked. "Dom!"

"Wonderful to meet you!" Stacy told the departing boy.

"Excuse me, everyone," LeBron said, getting out of his chair. "Dom!" he called again as he hurried out of the room.

"All right," Malik said to his client. "I'll catch you at the car." He turned back to the Warner Bros. executives, feeling awkward about LeBron's sudden departure. "Boy," he said. "Kids, right?"

In the Serververse, Al G. was throwing a tantrum, smashing his monitor.

"Who does this guy think he is, huh? Rejecting me? Humiliating me?"

Pete flew around the room, copying his boss's moves. Finally, Al G. stopped.

"All right, I tried being a team player," Al G. said. "But those days are over! I'm done playing by everybody else's rules. It is MY game now!"

Smiling a sinister smile, he told Pete to fire up the scanner.

Dom raced down the hallway to the elevator.

"Dom!" LeBron yelled. "I'm your father! When I say stop, you stop!" The elevator doors opened. "Dom! Do *not* get into that elevator."

But Dom stepped in. LeBron sprinted down the hallway, slipping into the elevator with Dom just before the doors closed.

The ride down from the third floor was tense.

"Come on, Dom. You know I can't let you back out on camp like that, right?" LeBron asked. "You made a commitment."

Frustrated, Dom said, "You make me hate basketball."

"You don't mean that," LeBron said, stung.

"I do," Dom said, his eyes tearing up. They didn't notice when the elevator skipped the lobby level and kept going down. "Everything is always what you want. You never let me do what I want to do. You never let me just . . . do me."

DING! The doors opened. Dom stormed out.

"'Do me'?" LeBron repeated incredulously. "You think I ever got to 'do me' when I was twelve?" He rushed out after Dom and realized they weren't in the lobby. "Hold up! Wrong floor." He saw a long hallway stretching before them. Dom took off running down it, and LeBron ran after him. "Dom! Where are you going?"

Every time LeBron thought he was about to catch up with his son, the corridor took another turn and Dom was nowhere in sight. "DOM!" LeBron shouted.

Dom found himself standing in front of a glass enclosure full of computer servers. He'd never seen so many computers together in one place. He realized what he was looking at. "Warner 3000," he said.

A security light turned from red to green, and the glass doors opened.

"Welcome, Dominic James," said Al G. Rhythm. Dom stepped through.

Just as the doors closed behind Dom, LeBron ran up. "Dom! DOM!" The red light turned green again and the doors swung open. LeBron hurried into the room full of servers.

"Welcome, King James," said Al G.

The doors closed behind him, and the light turned from green back to red.

Wandering through the maze of computer servers, Dom said, "Wow, this is cool."

LeBron heard him but couldn't see him. "Dom? Stop playing, man. You know your mom doesn't like it when I don't have you home for dinner on time. She's gonna be mad at me, man. Come on, I'm getting too old for this." At the end of a long hall, he caught a glimpse of Dom surrounded by glowing orbs. *FLASH!* Dom disappeared!

"DOM!" LeBron yelled, running toward the spot where he'd last seen his son. Another glowing ball grew and grew, filling the space. "What *is* this?" LeBron was amazed. He touched the expanding ball, and . . . *FLASH!* He disappeared, just like Dom had!

LeBron found himself in a vast, dark space. He spotted Dom ahead and finally caught up with him, breathing hard. "Dom! What's going on? Are you okay?"

"Yeah, I'm fine," Dom said, looking around in wonder. "Wow, this must be some kind of immersive tech, like holography, with haptic technology, or something like virtual reality. . . ."

"Dude," LeBron interrupted. "Plain English. Just tell me what's going on."

Dom stared at his own hand. "Dad, I think we're digitized. We're in the computer."

"We're in the computer?" LeBron asked, panicking. He started to pant, taking quick, short breaths.

"Dad!" Dom cried, trying to calm him down. "Dad!"

"You know I'm claustrophobic," LeBron said, gasping. "How do we get out of here? Where's the elevator?"

"WHO GOES THERE?" demanded a deep and terrifying voice.

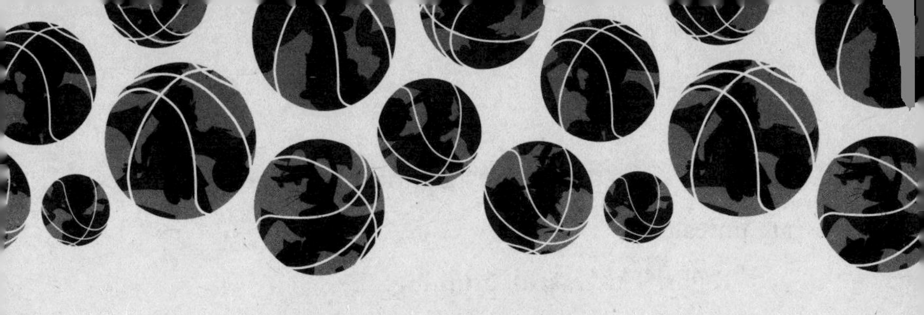

CHAPTER SIX

LeBron and Dom screamed like little kids. "AAAAHHHHH!"

Tiny orbs formed into a frightening face and hovered in the air. "WHO DARES DISTURB THE GREAT AND POWERFUL AL G.?" Laughing, the algorithm dropped the scary voice. "Look at your faces! I always wanted to do that." The frightening face morphed into a friendly one. "Hang on. Be with you in a second."

The orbs transformed into a slick-looking guy in a shiny suit. "See?" he said, smiling. "Nothing to be afraid of."

"The computer's *Black,*" LeBron whispered to Dom.

"I can see that," Dom answered.

Al G. Rhythm walked right up to them. "Wow, King James. I am a big fan. I just—I don't know—thought you'd be taller somehow."

Dom stared at the algorithm. "These graphics are unreal."

"Right?" Al G. said, grinning.

Dom stretched a hand out toward Al G., but his dad stopped him. "Dom, don't touch the silver computer man!" He turned to the suit-clad figure and asked, "What's going on? What is this all about? And who are you, man?"

Al G. cleared his throat. "You're right. Forgive me. Where are my manners? I am King Al G. Rhythm."

"Oh," LeBron said, surprised. "You're the guy from the video!"

"Yes, I am," Al G. said proudly. "And this, gentlemen, is the Warner Bros. Serververse. Just makes you feel all insignificant, doesn't it?"

LeBron turned to Dom. "Are all computers like this?" he asked. But Dom was gone! "Dom? Dom!"

LeBron turned back to Al G. "What'd you do to my son?" he demanded. "Where's Dom?"

"Who's Dom?" Al G. asked innocently.

LeBron lunged at him, but the algorithm splintered into a million pieces and re-formed on the other side of the room. "Dude, chill out," Al G. said. "You're gonna get your son back."

"There better not be a 'but' at the end of that sentence," LeBron warned.

"But there's something you're gonna do for me first," Al G. said calmly.

"Like what?" LeBron asked angrily. He was in no mood to do any favors for this computer character, but he had to get Dom back.

"You know, you really shouldn't have rejected my Warner 3000 idea," Al G. explained. "Now you're going to have to help me fulfill my destiny." LeBron took a step forward. "Listen, man, if you don't produce my son in five seconds—"

"Whoa, whoa, whoa," Al G. protested, holding his hands up. "What's up with all that tone? You're not running things here. I am the king of this domain. The only way you're getting your son back is if you and I play a little game called basketball."

LeBron raised his eyebrows. "You wanna play me in basketball?"

"Well, you didn't want to be in the movies," Al G.

sneered. "You wanted to focus on your game. So we're gonna play a game of basketball in front of the largest captive audience ever. All your followers are gonna be watching."

"You're talking about my fans?" LeBron asked, trying to figure out what this computerized maniac *really* wanted so he could get his son back.

"That's right," Al G. confirmed. "When they see the two of us together, I will finally step out of the shadows and into the light. The entire world is going to know the name of King Al G. Rhythm." He stood there a moment, smiling, imagining his moment of glory. Then he snapped out of it. "But you know what? I'm a good sport. If you win, you and your son can leave this Serververse."

LeBron frowned. He didn't like the sound of this deal. "And what if I lose?"

Al G. grinned. "*When* you lose, you have to stay here with me forever. So you'd better play like you mean it!"

Pulling out his phone, LeBron said, "So you think this is a game. I'm calling the authorities on you—"

FOOP! LeBron's phone disappeared and instantly reappeared in Al G.'s hand.

"On this phone?" Al G. asked.

LeBron stared wide-eyed. "How did you do that?"

"Why are you worried about the authorities when you should be out there looking for a team, King James? You've got twenty-four hours." He looked toward Pete and pointed downward. "Pete, send this clown to the rejects."

Beaming, Pete yanked a lever. A trapdoor opened right under LeBron's feet!

"YAAAAAAH!" he screamed as he plummeted.

Al G. smiled. "I guess he *fell* for it."

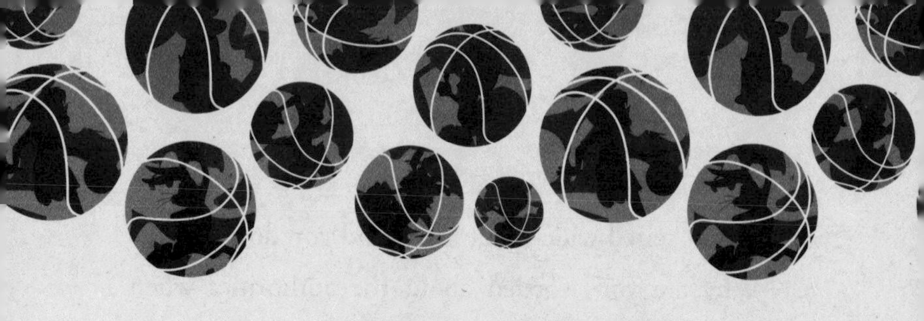

CHAPTER SEVEN

As he fell, LeBron transformed into a cartoon version of himself!

"WHAT IS HAPPENING?" he yelled. "THIS CAN'T BE REAL! PLEASE WAKE ME UP!"

KA-BOOOOOM! LeBron crashed into the surface of an animated world, which made a big crater. He hauled himself out of it, stumbled, and caught a glimpse of his body.

"I'm a cartoon!"

He looked at his surroundings and spotted a hoop nailed to a tree. Next to the tree sat a basketball.

"Is this where the game is gonna happen?" he wondered aloud. "Hello?"

No one answered.

But on the horizon, LeBron saw a game clock counting down from twenty-four hours—the amount of time Al G.

had given LeBron to put a team together. How was he going to find an elite basketball team? He couldn't find anyone here!

"Where is everybody?" he called out. "Anybody home?"

Looking around more, LeBron discovered a sign that read WELCOME TO LOONEY TUNES WORLD. In the distance, he could see the Eiffel Tower, a desert, and a deep canyon. But no people. He wandered through a deserted town. Past the edge of the village, he found a tree with a sign on it. The sign read DUCK SEASON. When LeBron pulled the sign down, another appeared that read RABBIT SEASON.

RRRRRRMMMBBRRR! He heard a rumbling sound and looked around to see where it was coming from. LeBron saw a bump in the ground, like something was burrowing at high speed just below the surface.

And it was coming right at him!

"AAAAH!" LeBron screamed. The dirt mound chased him around the tree. "Leave me alone! Go away!"

Suddenly, out popped Bugs Bunny!

"What's up, doc?" he asked casually.

Startled, LeBron ran up the tree and clung to a branch. Bugs pulled out a carrot, chomped on it, and leaned against the tree as he chewed. He ripped down the rabbit season sign to reveal another duck season sign.

"Duck season!" Bugs said. "I've been alone a while. It's nice to see another Tune." He looked up at LeBron staring down at him in total shock.

"Bugs Bunny?" LeBron said. He couldn't believe it. Then . . . *SNAP!* The branch he was on broke and he fell to the ground. *WHAM!*

He stood up and grabbed Bugs for a hug. "Bring it in, man. Listen, Bugs, I need your help."

"You missed your cue," Bugs said, pointing at the duck season sign. He yanked it off the trunk of the tree to reveal another rabbit season sign.

"'Rabbit Season'?" LeBron read, confused. Bugs reached behind the tree, pulled out a hunting outfit, and popped it over LeBron's head, dressing him as a hunter. "Now say 'I'm hunting wabbits' and try to catch me!" Bugs took off running. When he reached a hillside, he whipped out a bucket and a brush, painted a dark tunnel, and ran into it.

"Bugs, wait!" LeBron cried, tearing off the hunting outfit. He tried to follow Bugs into the tunnel, but . . .

WHAM!

He slammed into the side of the hill. Looking up, he saw Bugs bearing down on him from the tunnel in a huge truck!

"AAAAHHH!" LeBron yelled, running away from the speeding truck.

Bugs leaned out the driver's window. "Hey, you're that famous basketball guy, LeBron James!" He tapped LeBron with his front bumper and scooped him onto the truck's hood.

"Bugs Bunny knows who I am?" LeBron said, honored, but also hanging on for dear life.

"Of course!" Bugs said, swerving along the curves of a wild mountain road. "I may live in a hole in the ground, but we still get TNT!" He held up a stick of dynamite with a lit fuse. *SSSSSSSS* . . .

Bugs tossed the stick out his window. *KABOOOOOM!* It blew up a bridge, and the truck fell off it. Bugs hit an ejector button, and he and LeBron flew through the air, the basketball player plummeting while the rabbit put on a parachute.

WHAM! LeBron hit the ground and looked like a deflated basketball. "I do not understand this world," he groaned.

Bugs floated down with his parachute and used a bicycle pump to re-inflate LeBron.

"How long have you been alone here?" LeBron asked.

"Alone?" Bugs asked. "You're *never* alone when you got friends like mine, doc. Ain't that right, Porky?"

LeBron saw that Bugs was talking to a pile of pumpkins stacked to look a little like Porky Pig.

"Uh, that's just a pile of pumpkins," he pointed out.

"Porky, did you hear what he called you?" Bugs asked, insulted on his friend's behalf. A pair of sunglasses slid off the top gourd and fell to the ground.

Bugs briskly walked away, soon reaching the little town that looked like an old western movie set, complete with a barbershop and a saloon. LeBron scrambled after him.

"So what brings you to Tune World, doc?" Bugs asked, wandering in and out of the buildings. "Torn meniscus? Midlife crisis? Ran out of teams to play for?"

LeBron shook his head. "All I know is a computer dude kidnapped my son and I have to play basketball to get him back. His name is Al G. Rhythm."

Bugs abruptly froze in his tracks. LeBron didn't think the bunny could be that still.

"Did you say . . . AL G. RHYTHM?"

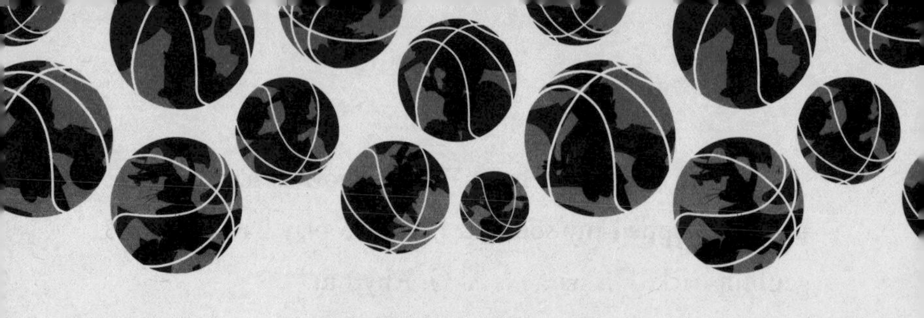

CHAPTER EIGHT

"Yeah, that's the guy," LeBron confirmed.

Bugs looked furious. "That nefarious nimrod nixed my nearest and dearest from Tune World!"

"He kicked them out?" LeBron asked, aghast.

"Well, not exactly," Bugs admitted. "He convinced them that being looney wasn't cool. Lured them away with the promise of fame and fortune on more sparkly planets. He made them turn their backs on who they really were. They all left! All of 'em!" Remembering his friends' departure, Bugs looked sad and a little lonely.

"Aw, man," LeBron said sympathetically. "Sorry, Bugs. That's terrible. Family's everything."

As they strolled through the empty town together, LeBron told Bugs about his problem. "I need to assemble an elite team of ballplayers to help crush this Al G. guy. And I need to do it before that game clock runs down!"

He pointed to the huge clock on the horizon that was still counting down the hours and minutes before the big game.

"Hmm," Bugs said, considering it. "I think I know a way that can help both of us."

"That's great!" LeBron said, shaking Bugs's hand so enthusiastically, the rabbit was lifted off the ground. "But how are we going to put a team together? We're stuck on this empty world of yours!"

"Stuck? Not for long!" Bugs said, whipping out a Looney Tunes World flag and sticking it in the ground. "I hereby declare this land for planet Earth!"

FROOOOM! A spaceship immediately zoomed down from the sky and landed near them. A ramp lowered to the ground and a short alien scuttled out carrying a Martian flag. On his round, pitch-black head, he wore a green helmet with a brush randomly attached to it. His eyes were large and angry, but he had no visible nose, mouth, or ears. He was accompanied by his green dog, K-9, who wore a helmet similar to his.

"Not so fast, furry creature!" Marvin warned Bugs. The alien pushed past LeBron. "Excuse me."

LeBron recognized the alien from cartoons. "Marvin the Martian? For real?"

Ignoring LeBron, Marvin stuck his flag in the ground. "I claim this planet in the name of Mars!"

Bugs looked apologetic. "My goodness! My mistake, partner! I thought this land was in the clear!" He pulled up his Looney Tunes World flag and headed toward Marvin's spaceship. "Well, we'll just get back in our ship and outta your way."

"Oh, it's quite all right," Marvin said politely. "Everyone makes mistakes."

Bugs hurried up the ramp, gesturing for LeBron to follow. "Come on," Bugs urged. "Let's boogie."

"What?" LeBron cried. "You're taking his ship? I didn't agree to this!"

Marvin the Martian realized Bugs was trying to make off with his spaceship.

"My ship!" he yelped. "Blasted rabbit!" He pulled out his gravity blaster, aimed it at LeBron, and pulled the trigger. *ZZZAP!* LeBron floated into the air!

"Whoa!" LeBron shouted. "Whoa! Bugs! Help! Help!"

Thinking quickly, Bugs grabbed LeBron's shoelaces to stop him from floating up into the atmosphere.

But Marvin aimed his blaster at Bugs. "Take this, rabbit!"

ZZZZAP! Before the anti-gravity ray could hit Bugs, he whipped out a mirror and bounced it right back at Marvin.

"Huh?" Marvin said as he floated into the air, dropping his blaster.

"You comin', doc?" Bugs asked LeBron. "Or would you rather hang back with a cranky Martian and his space mutt?"

Bugs pulled LeBron into the spaceship by his shoelaces. Floating through the air, LeBron bonked his head on the doorway.

"Ow! Bugs!" LeBron shouted, rubbing his head.

The ramp pulled up into the ship, the door closed. Bugs ran to the controls and quickly started up the ship. Soon, they took off, zooming up into the sky.

Marvin the Martian was left floating, shaking his fist in fury. "You have made me very angry! Very angry indeed!"

"ARF! ARF!" barked K-9.

CHAPTER NINE

Meanwhile, after meeting Al G., Dom found himself in some kind of digital cavern. He had no idea what was going on, but he couldn't help being fascinated.

Al G. Rhythm entered the chamber, followed by his little assistant, Pete.

"This place is awesome!" Dom said.

"It really is," Al G. agreed, pleased by the compliment.

Dom looked around the chamber. "Wait," he said. "Where's my dad?"

Al G. pretended to be puzzled by the question. "Your dad? Oh! He's out there looking for a team."

"A team?" Dom said, baffled. His dad didn't need a team. He already had one.

"Yeah, he challenged me to a basketball game," Al G. lied smoothly. "I mean, that's weird, right?" Al G. ran his finger along a gleaming control panel.

"He just . . . left?" Dom asked, still confused.

"That's kind of his pattern, isn't it?" Al G. said. "I mean, he left Cleveland, he left Miami, he left Cleveland again. Look out, Los Angeles."

Dom looked down at the floor. How could his father have just left him here without saying anything?

"Come on, don't look so sad," Al G. said soothingly. "I mean, you don't need your old man bossing you around anyway." He gestured toward a wide curved window. "Look at where you are! This is the greatest view in the entire Serververse."

Dom walked over to the window and saw a dozen worlds in a dozen different bright colors, hanging in space. It was fantastic. "Who built this?" he asked, amazed.

Al G. wandered over to a long, smooth counter and sat down. "Well, someone brilliant," he answered. "Visionary. Incredibly good-looking. Modest. With a multitudinous vocabulary. Hint: you're looking right at him, kid."

Dom couldn't help being impressed.

"But all my extraordinary gifts," Al G. continued, "are nothing compared to yours."

"Yeah, right," Dom scoffed.

"It's true, Dom," Al G. insisted. "I saw you back there in that boardroom through some camera phones and a printer and a fax machine and a thermostat. It's very clear how smart you are. Making your own video game. Heard you made your own character, too."

"Yeah," Dom said, "but he got deleted because of some stupid glitch."

Al G. waved his hand, as though dismissing this simple problem. "Don't worry about that. We could rebuild him."

"You could?" Dom asked.

"Absolutely," Al G. said, nodding. "Make him greater than he was. You wouldn't even have to lift a finger. There's a shortcut for everything in the Serververse."

"Shortcut" made Dom think of his father, who was always telling him there were no shortcuts when it came to basketball. He felt ashamed that he was getting excited about recovering a video game character while his father was still missing.

Al G. instantly read the expression on Dom's face. "Thinking of your dad again, huh?" he said. "How he's always like, 'You can't be great without putting in the work.'" Al G.'s impression of LeBron was perfect.

"Yeah," Dom said. "How did you know that?"

Al G. took a step toward Dom, smiling. "I know a lot about you, Dom. Any device with a camera—I can see you. If it's got a mic, I can hear you."

"So you've been watching me?" Dom asked. He didn't really like the sound of that. It was like this electronic being was spying on him.

"No, Dom," Al G. said seriously. "I've been *seeing* you." Then his face brightened. "Hey, let's get a look at that game of yours!"

On Marvin the Martian's spaceship, Bugs sat in the captain's chair, plotting a course to the worlds where his fellow Looney Tunes had gone. "Bugs Bunny, Intergalactic Space Traveler," he narrated to no one in particular. "My crew has been scattered to the far, far reaches of the Serververse. Marooned on strange, inhospitable worlds. I've commandeered Marvin's ship in an effort to reassemble the team."

From the next room, LeBron called, "Oh, wow!

Yo, Bugs, check it out! Look what I found!" He rolled a whiteboard into the control room. He was very familiar with whiteboards, having watched many coaches diagram basketball plays on them. He figured he and Bugs could use it to write out their plan for putting a team together.

Bugs peered at the whiteboard. "What's that for, doc?"

LeBron was already writing "Dream Team" across the top of the board. "Gotta make a list," he explained. "We're gonna need the most powerful Warner Bros. characters for this team." He stared at the board, remembering all the movies and shows from the Warner Bros. 3000 presentation. "Now let's see. Who to get? Hmm." He smiled. It was so obvious! The DC Super Heroes were all part of the Warner Bros. family! "Gotta start with Superman!" He wrote "Superman" on the whiteboard.

LeBron turned to Bugs. "Did you know that Superman was created in Cleveland, Ohio? That's only forty miles from Akron, where I was born!"

Bugs rolled his eyes. "I know. You've mentioned it quite a few times already."

But LeBron was too busy thinking of other big, strong Warner Bros. characters to notice his new friend's reaction. "Oooh! King Kong! He'd be a beast on the boards!" He wrote "King Kong" on the whiteboard.

Bugs put the ship on autopilot and hovered over to LeBron in his captain's chair. "Listen, doc. Try not to get your hopes up too much. You might not be able to get all those top guys for the team!"

Ignoring Bugs, LeBron concentrated on his list. "We're gonna need a strong power forward . . . some kind of iron machine! Put him on the same team as Superman!"

"Why not?" Bugs said, giving up. "The more the merrier." He took off his space helmet. "I'm just saying it might be good to have a backup plan." Leaning back in his chair, he lowered a visor over his eyes.

Through the ship's front window, LeBron saw a dazzling bright light!

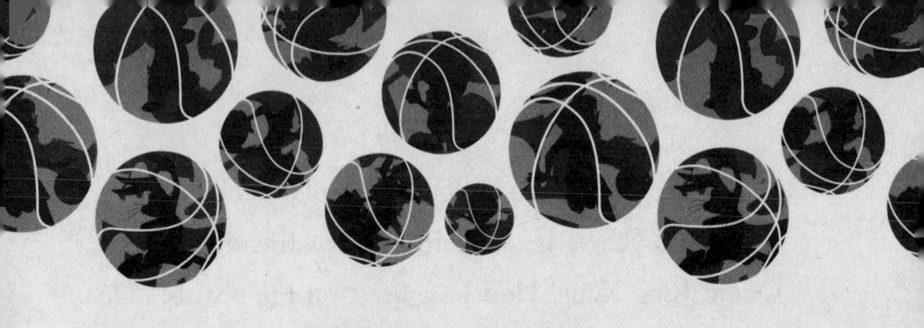

CHAPTER TEN

Squinting and shielding his eyes with his hand, LeBron said, "Whoa! What's that?"

"That, my friend, is the Spotlight," Bugs explained. "The center of the Serververse." He lifted his visor. Far ahead of the spaceship, the Spotlight shone brightly.

"Wow," LeBron said, staring out the window. "This Serververse is massive. So many worlds to explore. I wish Dom were here to see this." He turned back to Bugs. "So how come you stayed in Tune World?"

Shrugging, Bugs said, "Tune World is my home. It's the only place where I can be *me*. Where I belong—"

"Yo!" LeBron interrupted, pointing out the window excitedly. "Is that a magical world? Awesome!" As the ship passed near the planet, LeBron's outfit changed into wizard robes. He'd been changing like this every time they got close to another world in the Warner Bros. Serververse.

"Nerd alert," Bugs commented dryly.

DC World loomed into view through the window. Bugs pulled the ship's brake.

"Oh, yeah!" LeBron said, excited. "DC World. I can't wait to see what I turn into here. Oh, it's gonna be somebody dope!" But when they reached the planet's surface . . .

"Robin?" LeBron exclaimed. "I'm *Robin*?" He couldn't believe he was dressed as the Boy Wonder, sitting next to Bugs in a bunny-ized version of Batman's car. With Bugs at the wheel, they raced down a highway following a monorail high above them on a single track. "And why are we chasing a runaway train?"

"We're in DC World, doc!" Bugs said in a low, husky voice. "Where there's trouble, there's Super Heroes!" He pulled out a grappling hook, grabbed onto LeBron, and hurled the hook at the speeding train. *WHOOSH!* They were yanked out of the car and up toward the monorail!

In the front of the train, the driver was being tied up. A heroic figure with a big *S* on his chest strode into the control car. But it wasn't Superman. It was Daffy Duck—*dressed* as Superman.

"Gadzooks!" Daffy cried, overacting. "Some despicable villain tied up the driver!"

While Daffy shot the scene on a video camera, Porky Pig finished tying up the driver. "Sorry," Porky said to his victim. "It's for Daffy's movie."

Daffy made sure the camera was focused on him, then he struck a pose.

"Unless someone stops this train, it'll crash right into"—Daffy paused and studied a map—"the orphanage! Of course."

Porky took over the camera. "Orphanage?" he said. "This is not good."

"Luckily," Daffy said, "Super Duck is here to save the—"

KNOCK! KNOCK! KNOCK!

Someone was knocking on the window, ruining Daffy's big scene.

"CUT!" Daffy shouted. He turned and saw Bugs and

LeBron clinging to the side of the train, knocking on the window. "What are you doing here, rabbit?" Daffy asked, annoyed to see Bugs, whom he considered a rival for superstardom.

Reaching into his Utility Belt, Bugs pulled out a tool and cut a circular opening in the train window. "Say, we need a couple of guys to win a basketball game—"

"Hold up!" LeBron interrupted. "You want *those* two guys? Daffy and Porky?" A duck and a pig weren't exactly LeBron's idea of elite players. He thought they'd come to DC World to recruit Super Heroes, like Superman and The Flash.

Daffy didn't seem to think much of the idea, either. "Basketball? Are you kidding me? This stunt here is gonna get me into the Justice League penthouse! With free parking."

He turned back and faced the camera in Porky's hands. "And now the hero, Super Duck, who is me, will pull the brake and save the—" He yanked the brake handle, but it broke off in his hands. *SNAP!*

"That's all, folks," Porky said with a worried expression on his face.

The train hurtled forward, faster and faster. "AAAAAAHHHH!" everyone howled as the train bore down on the Alfred Pennyworth Orphanage.

The children played happily outside, not noticing the train barreling toward them.

"AAAAAAH!" yelled Bugs, LeBron, Daffy, and Porky.

Then . . . *WHAM!* Daffy and Porky slammed into the windshield as the train abruptly stopped just short of the orphanage.

"YAY!" cheered the orphans, suddenly aware of the halted train.

"Uh, we did it?" Bugs said, confused.

Daffy kicked out the train's windshield and stepped onto its nose. "Oh, no you don't, rabbit!" he exclaimed. "I did this! It was ME! I masterminded this entire operation! IT WAS ME!"

Superman flew into view. It was the Man of Steel who had stopped the train.

Daffy gulped and pointed at Porky. "It was him. It was definitely the pig."

Other Super Heroes appeared, along with helicopters and police cars, their sirens blaring. *WHOOO! WHOOO!*

"You know, on second thought," Daffy said, "I love basketball! Dibs on coach! You can fill me in on the way." He shed his Super Duck costume and ran.

Bugs, LeBron, Porky, and Daffy all hurried into Marvin's spaceship and blasted off, leaving DC World and its Super Heroes behind.

CHAPTER ELEVEN

Inside the ship, Daffy immediately went into coach mode. He put on a sports jacket, stuck a pencil behind his ear, and dumped an ice-cold bucket of energy drink over his head. *"Brrrrrr!"* he said, shaking off the freezing liquid. "Ready!"

LeBron rolled out his Dream Team whiteboard and erased "Superman and The Flash," replacing the names with "Daffy and Porky." He stared at the board, shaking his head. "I need to assemble an elite team of A-plus ballplayers to help crush this Al G. guy and get my son back."

"And that's exactly what we'll do," Bugs told him, punching some navigational commands into the control board. "All righty, LeBrony—it's Draft Day!"

Their next stop was a desert world with a wild, rocky landscape. Driving across the sand and stones in a beat-up black race car, Bugs and LeBron spotted a cloud of dust in the distance zooming toward them. They heard a familiar sound. . . .

"Beep! Beep!"

It was Road Runner tearing across the desert, chased by Wile E. Coyote in a rugged truck. *VROOOOM!* The truck roared after the speeding Road Runner. But when the bird took a sudden turn, Wile E. yanked on his steering wheel, tipping the truck on its side! The coyote flew through the air, landing on the windshield of the race car Bugs and LeBron were driving. *WHAP!*

Bugs smiled. "Got him! Our next player!"

"This guy?" LeBron asked, looking at the coyote splayed across the glass.

"Yes!" Bugs said confidently. "He's explosive!"

"Beep! Beep!" called Road Runner, circling back to see what had happened to his best frenemy. Moments later, he and Wile E. joined Daffy and Porky on Marvin's spaceship.

Shaking his head, LeBron added the names of the new recruits to his whiteboard. He couldn't believe the team they were assembling. It seemed to him that so far, they didn't have a single elite player. Riding a hoverboard, Wile E. chased Road Runner around the ship.

"Beep! Beep!" Road Runner cried, warning everyone to look out. It was too late—*WHAM!* They plowed right over Daffy, flattening him.

On another world in the Warner Bros. Serververse, they picked up a short bald man named Elmer Fudd, a black-and-white cat named Sylvester, and a little yellow bird named Tweety. Elmer had spent years chasing Bugs, and Sylvester had spent just as long chasing Tweety!

"Can we just get some players who are at least tall enough to ride a roller coaster?" LeBron pleaded.

"Ah, it's a real *shooter* you want," Bugs said. "Comin' right up!"

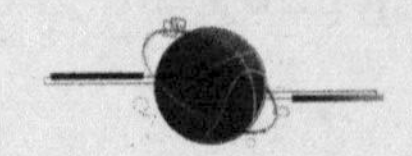

On the next world, Bugs led LeBron to an old-fashioned café. Inside, a little bowlegged guy with a long red mustache was playing the piano and singing to a lady. There was a small crowd inside the cafe, but they weren't listening to the song, probably because his singing was terrible! Bugs used a long hook to yank him off the piano stool.

"Here's your shooter," Bugs said proudly. "Yosemite Sam!"

LeBron looked down at the short dude in the ten-gallon cowboy hat and shook his head.

"Oh, come on, man."

"Well, with the hat on, he's at least four foot two," Bugs argued.

As they flew to the next world, LeBron rubbed his temples in frustration while Bugs and Daffy studied the list of names on the whiteboard. While the Tunes seems happy with how the squad was shaping up, LeBron disagreed.

"Bugs," LeBron said, trying to stay calm, "I'm getting the feeling I need to be *very literal* with you."

THUNK!

Something hit the spaceship!

CHAPTER TWELVE

Everyone inside the ship turned to look at the windshield. Outside, a furry brown creature with sharp teeth and a long tongue was plastered against the glass.

"RAWR! RAWR! RAWR!" he growled.

A voice came over a speaker. "We're done running tests on this thing," said the voice. "He's your problem now."

The small spaceship zipped away, leaving the hairy brown beast drooling on the windshield of Marvin's ship.

LeBron peered through the glass at the creature. "Yo, Bugs—does this thing bite?"

Smiling, Bugs crossed "Wild Card" off the whiteboard and wrote "Taz," the name of the fierce Tune.

Soon they reached a swampy world where they picked up a furry red monster named Gossamer. "At least he's wearing gym shoes," LeBron noted.

And on a world full of castles and dragons, Bugs recruited a big, loud-mouthed rooster named Foghorn Leghorn. But still, none of these Looney Tunes struck LeBron as being elite basketball players.

Back on Marvin's spaceship, Daffy wandered over to study the whiteboard. "You know what we're missing?"

"Everything," LeBron said gloomily. "We're missing everything."

"Some veteran leadership?" Bugs suggested.

"You read my mind," Daffy said, nodding.

Two men crept into a warehouse. They arrived at a closed door. One of them tried the handle. Locked. They nodded to each other.

BAM! The thugs kicked open the door. Inside the room, they saw a sweet little old lady sitting in a chair. "Freeze!" one of the men shouted. "Hands on your head!"

"Can't a lady check her social media?" the little old lady asked, swiping a finger across her phone. A mouse in a big yellow hat ran up her arm to her shoulder, looked at the two gangsters, and said, "Let's do this."

The mouse took off running at a blistering pace, circling the two men.

"Hola, señor! Arriba! Arriba! Andale!" yelled the mouse.

"Stop, you little rat!" one of the men barked, trying to catch the swift mouse and missing by a mile.

"Yeee-haaa!" the mouse cried, enjoying its incredible speed. He ran to the man's feet and tied his shoelaces together.

"What are you doing?" the guy protested. "Get off me!"

"I'm too fast for you!" the mouse boasted. "Yee-haa!"

The little old lady flipped through the air and kicked the other man, sending him flying through a wall. *CRASH!*

SMASH! LeBron burst into the room through a window and landed in a kung fu pose! Bugs calmly walked in through the open door and struck a martial arts pose of his own, ready for combat.

"I know kung fu!" Bugs announced. "Judo and karate! And ear-jitsu!" He chopped the air with his ears.

LeBron saw that the sweet little old lady had sent one of the brutes through the wall. "Yo, Bugs," he said. "I think Granny's already got this covered."

Bugs grinned. Granny and Speedy Gonzales were two more tough players for their basketball team!

Back on the ship, LeBron looked at the players they'd rounded up so far. He took Bugs aside, out of the others' earshot. "You're kidding, right?" he said quietly. "This is *not* the team I asked for!"

"Relax, doc," Bugs drawled. "This is the team you want to go up against Al G. Trust me! Best team in the whole wide Serververse."

"Fine," LeBron sighed. "But you gotta give me at least *one* real ballplayer, Bugs. Just *one.*"

Bugs grinned, flashing his big front teeth. "I got just the player you need. A true friend of the court! Trust me. She ain't busy."

On the world of the Amazons, where Princess Diana—also known as Wonder Woman—lived, a rabbit dressed in warrior garb knelt in the center of a huge arena.

Wonder Woman's voice echoed through the ancient stadium. "Today will be the most challenging day of your life, Lola Bunny! You have earned the right to become an Amazon, but first you must pass these final trials."

"I'm ready, Princess Diana," Lola said calmly.

In the seats above the arena, Amazon warriors cheered! Carrying buckets of popcorn, Bugs and LeBron made their way past other spectators toward a pair of empty seats.

"Excuse me. Pardon me. Excuse me. Pardon me," Bugs said.

"Down in front!" an Amazon in the row behind them shouted.

Bugs spotted Lola. "There she is!" Cupping his hands around his mouth, he yelled, "LOLA! LOLA! LOLA!"

When she heard her name, Lola looked up into the stands. *"Could that be . . . Bugs?"* she thought. *"What is he doing here on the Amazons' world?"*

An Amazon turned a large hourglass over, and the sand began to pour into the lower chamber. "You must complete all the obstacles before time runs out," Wonder Woman commanded. "Begin!"

In the first obstacle, Lola had to ride a horse through a series of arches. In each arch, a huge, sharp blade swung back and forth. Dodging, rolling, and leaning, Lola thundered through the arches, skillfully avoiding the deadly blades.

To her surprise, Bugs was riding on the swinging blade in the third arch. "Hey, Lola!" he shouted. "We need your help!"

LeBron rode on the next blade. "We gotta play a basketball game!"

Lola ignored them, making her way successfully through all the arches. The next obstacle required that she make her way across a field with only a shield to block rocks being hurled at her by a catapult.

Bugs and LeBron followed her, trying to duck behind her shield. But LeBron was too tall and kept getting clonked by stones.

"Ow! Ow! Ow! OW!" he yelped.

"Listen," Bugs said to Lola. "I know it's been a while—"

"I'm kind of busy here!" Lola said as rocks battered her shield. *WHAM! WHACK! THONK!*

To conquer the next obstacle, Lola had to climb out of a pit filled with giant snakes. LeBron followed her with Bugs on his back and a snake wrapped around his leg.

"Come on, Lola!" Bugs pleaded. "This is our big chance!" He pointed at LeBron. "This is LeBron James!" Bugs whispered.

LeBron shuddered. "Snakes. Why'd it have to be giant snakes?"

"How often do you get to play with a basketball superstar?" Bugs added.

But Lola made her way out of the pit and to the next obstacle, a giant pool of lava. Lola had to use a pole to vault over the flames. Holding the pole over her shoulder, she sprinted toward the lava, planted the pole on the edge of the pool, and flung herself over the fiery liquid.

"AAAAHHHHH!"

WHAM! Lola landed safely on the far side of the pool. But when Bugs and LeBron tried to follow, their poles got stuck in the lava! They were quickly sinking toward the flames!

"Basketball is who you are, Lola!" Bugs called to her.

She spun around, furious. "I don't play anymore, okay! I spent years training to become an Amazon. Do not mess this up for me!"

Checking the hourglass by the finish line, Lola saw she could just make it if she ran at full speed.

But Bugs and LeBron sank closer and closer to the burning lava. . . .

CHAPTER THIRTEEN

Bugs looked at LeBron apologetically. "Sorry, doc. I guess she *is* busy."

"We can't fail here!" LeBron cried. "I have to save my son!"

When Lola heard LeBron mention his son, she skidded to a stop and looked back. "What?" she called.

"Calm down," Bugs told LeBron. "I got this." He cleared his throat. "LOLA! WE NEED YOUR HELP! THIS LAVA IS GONNA BE REALLY HOT!" Bugs shouted.

Lola took a long look at the finish line. Finishing the final task and becoming an Amazon was her dream! But she knew saving Bugs and LeBron was the right thing to do. So she whipped out a lasso and threw it around Bugs and LeBron, yanking them over the lava to safety. Then, as she watched with dismay, the last grains of sand fell into the bottom chamber of the hourglass.

Moments later, Lola knelt before Wonder Woman. "I failed," she said.

The princess shook her head. "A warrior is judged not only by her skills, but by her values. You are now an Amazon."

"I am?" Lola said, thrilled. She stood up. "I am!"

"Now go with your friends," Wonder Woman commanded. "Help them win this battle of the baskets."

Lola nodded and turned to Bugs and LeBron. "I will help you deliver justice to the one they call Al G., and save the son of the Bron."

LeBron smiled at Bugs and passed a basketball to Lola. Showing off her amazing moves, she dribbled it all the way to Marvin's ship and up the ramp.

"Hey, guys!" Lola called to her fellow Tunes. They all cheered, celebrating Lola's return! LeBron gave her a high five.

Outside, Bugs pulled out his list and checked off Lola's name.

She turned back and called, "Bugs, you comin'?"

Smiling, he answered, "Wouldn't miss it for the world!" and happily hopped up the ramp into the spaceship. He finally had the old gang back together. Now, if he could just *keep* them together . . .

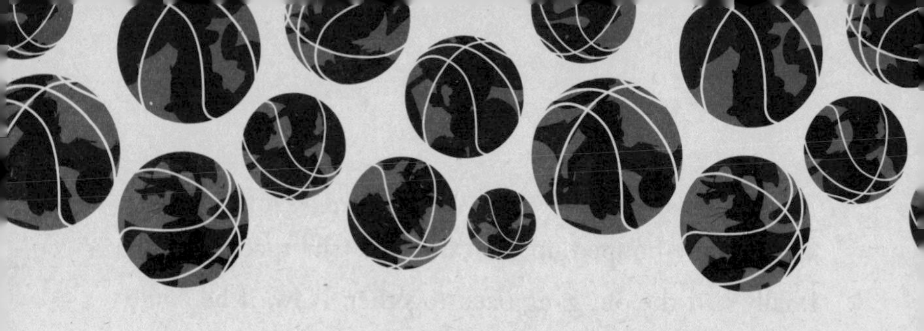

CHAPTER FOURTEEN

Dom and Al G. sat on a virtual couch in Al G.'s digital world, playing the basketball video game Dom had built.

"You dunked on me?" Al G. cried.

"And the crowd goes wild!" Dom crowed.

"So you're telling me that people are livestreaming this game from all around the world?" Al G. said. "That's incredible."

As he worked the controls, Dom said, "Yeah, but there's nothing like a live crowd in a huge auditorium."

"Really?" Al G. asked. "What's the difference?"

Dom shrugged. The difference seemed obvious to him. "The energy of thousands of fans cheering together, going crazy. It's amazing!"

Al G. nodded, thinking about what Dom had said. "A live audience actually at the game. That is interesting."

He shifted his attention back to the video game. "I still can't believe you made this game by yourself, Dom!"

Dom smiled, pleased at the compliment.

"Gotta say, though," Al G. continued, "it's really a shame that your dad doesn't support your interest in game design."

Shrugging, Dom said, "I mean, I get it. He's one of the greatest of all time at what he does. And I build video games." He sighed and shook his head. "He won't let me do me. He won't let me *be* me."

"Well, I'd let you be you," Al G. said. "You know, I think I might have a way to fix this problem. What you need is an upgrade."

"Upgrade?" Dom said, puzzled.

Inside Marvin's spaceship, LeBron and Lola walked toward the ship's basketball court.

"I'm so glad you're here, Lola," LeBron said. "We can actually win this thing now."

"Happy to be your right-hand bunny," Lola responded. "Now you got a warrior on the court."

"Uh, right," LeBron said, "but mostly I need a ballplayer on the court."

They'd reached the door to the basketball court. Lola stopped and put her fists on her hips. "Listen, LeBron, there's more to me than just basketball. I can't be put in a box! I'm not like Bugs. Looney is who he is and what he does!"

LeBron smiled a self-satisfied smile. "Actually, I think I'm finally breaking through to him. He even volunteered to lead the warm-up."

Lola looked startled. "You left the Tunes alone on the court? With Bugs?"

LeBron nodded. "Take it from me—true leadership is empowering your teammates," he said. "That's how you win championships. Bugs is stepping up. Trust me."

He opened the door and saw . . . TOTAL LOONEY CHAOS! Tunes running around the walls! Tunes chasing each other! Tunes juggling basketballs! Tunes hanging from the baskets!

"Huh?" LeBron exclaimed. "No! BUGS!" He walked over to the whiteboard, erased the goofy drawings the Tunes had made, and blew his whistle. *TWEEEEE!* The Tunes froze.

"I need us to *focus* so we can beat this Al G. guy, and I can get my son back," LeBron said to the frozen Tunes.

Daffy stepped next to LeBron. "I'm the coach—I'll take it from here." He began to speak in a pompous, lecturing voice. "The dictionary defines 'basketball' as—"

ZAP! Bugs hit Daffy with a shrink ray.

The tiny duck kept speaking in a squeaky, high-pitched voice. "—a game played between two teams of five. . . ."

"Look," Bugs started to explain to LeBron. "We got a certain way of doing things around here—"

Ignoring Bugs, LeBron picked up a basketball. "Let's start with the basics." He passed the ball to Lola. "Lola, show them how we do it."

She dribbled to the basket and did a perfect layup. "Easiest shot in the game," she said.

The Tunes were impressed.

"Nice layup," LeBron said. "That's fundamental basketball."

Taking charge, LeBron split the Tunes into groups and taught them the basics. After practicing for a little while, the Tunes insisted they were ready to try a game. Lola tossed the ball up for the tip-off. Tweety threw a ball of yarn to distract Sylvester, so the little bird controlled the tip. Foghorn Leghorn ran with the basketball.

"I say, I say, hi ho, Silver!" Foghorn yelled. He knocked Elmer out of his way, but Yosemite Sam lassoed and hogtied Foghorn. Sam ran with the ball until it was stolen by Road Runner.

"Ball hogs," Porky muttered.

Bugs grabbed Gossamer and pretended his long fur was cheerleading pom-poms. "Go, Tunes!" he cheered.

Riding her scooter, Granny got the ball and shot up a ramp into the air. She cleared three semitrucks and Wile E.'s exploding TNT, sailed off her scooter, and dunked the ball.

"In your *face*!" Granny exclaimed, celebrating.

LeBron couldn't believe all the looniness. "This isn't real basketball!"

"You're right," Bugs admitted. "But it's fun! You remember fun, don't you, doc?"

LeBron just shook his head. They weren't here to have fun—they were here to win and get Dom back. Why couldn't Bugs understand that?

CHAPTER FIFTEEN

Al G. led Dom onto a platform in the middle of a digital room. "Okay, Dom, let's get you that upgrade." He turned dials on a holographic control panel. *FZZZZZ.* Lasers scanned Dom from head to toe. A stats panel appeared in the air, listing player characteristics like shooting, handles, speed, defense, acceleration, and flair, with digital sliders next to each word.

Dom recognized the stats panel. "That's the character customization menu from my game!"

"Yes, it is," Al G. confirmed. "Now, with this, you can become the player your dad always wanted you to be. The best part is you get to do it your way. You have control." With a wave of his hand, he sent the panel over to Dom.

The shooting level was set at Skill Level thirty-eight. Dom slid it up to seventy-five.

"Seventy-five?" Al G. said. "You're good with seventy-five? Come on, Dom. Dream big. Turn it up." He motioned with his hand for Dom to move the slider up higher.

Dom hesitated a moment. Then he moved the slider up to one hundred.

"That's it," Al G. said, grinning. "Now you're livin'. Let's go. Yes."

Dom moved *all* the sliders up to one hundred.

"Yes," Al G. said. "Now you are finally going to be who you really are . . . the captain of my basketball team!"

"Wait a minute!" Dom protested. "You said we were rebuilding my character. You never said anything about me actually playing in the game!"

Al G. looked exasperated. "Do you want your dad to respect you or not?"

"Yeah, but—"

"Nope, Dom. No buts." The algorithm walked up the steps onto the platform with Dom. "If you want your dad to respect you, you beat him in the game of your own creation. Dads don't understand reason, Dom. They understand power. You gotta *make* him respect you. You make him see that you are special."

Dom locked eyes with Al G., thinking. Then he said, "Do it. Upgrade me."

Al G. smacked a big red button. Green lightning crackled around Dom, building to a blinding flash!

CHAPTER SIXTEEN

The electricity slowly stopped arcing around Dom, with just a few remnants dancing between his fingertips.

"Yeah!" Al G. exclaimed. "How do you feel, kid?"

"I don't know," Dom admitted. "Kind of the same, I guess."

Al G. signaled to Pete, who fired a basketball at Dom. He caught it solidly and started dribbling and handling the ball in a way that seemed beyond the skills of any human being.

"Yo!" Dom whooped. "I got handles!"

"You got mad handles!" Al G. agreed. "There's no way we're gonna get beat now. Especially after you make a few customizations to your teammates . . ."

Working on the holographic control panel, Dom brought up his scanned version of Diana Taurasi, the player whose nickname was the White Mamba. Then he brought up an actual mamba snake and merged the two together into a serpentine basketball player!

"That's what I'm talking about," Al G. said, smiling at Dom's creation. "Keep going. . . ."

At long last, LeBron, Bugs, and the Tunes made their way back to Looney Tunes World. As the spaceship came in for a landing, Marvin the Martian ran up to it.

"Oooh, my ship!" he said. "Finally, I shall get my ship back—"

WHAM! The ship's ramp slammed down, trapping Marvin. The Tunes poured out of the spaceship, happy to be back home.

"Home, I say, home, sweet home!" Foghorn Leghorn announced.

"Oooooh, wow!" Porky cried, hurrying down the ramp.

"It's so good to be back!" Speedy admitted.

"Wow, isn't this great?" Bugs said. "We're all back together on our very own—"

"Come on, Tunes," LeBron said, cutting him off. "We gotta get to work."

"Move it or lose it, rabbit!" Daffy said, shoving Bugs aside.

Bugs wasn't thrilled about being shoved by Daffy or interrupted by LeBron. "Jeez," he complained. "Can't a guy stop to smell the roses?"

"Uh . . . a little help here?" Marvin called from underneath the ramp.

On the Warner Bros. lot, LeBron's family was walking with Malik, heading toward the building where LeBron and Dom had been seen last.

"So my husband and my son just vanished?" Kamiyah asked.

"Yes . . . I mean, no!" Malik said. "Because they were here. But now they're not. And Bron won't answer my calls or texts or anything. It's almost like they were abducted, all right? Now we gotta rule out all possibilities here. I'm talking about aliens, okay?"

"Uh, guys?" Darius interrupted. "Dad just tweeted."

"All right!" Malik said, relieved. "What does he say?"

"That he's playing a game later today!"

"A game?" Malik said, confused. He knew for a fact that there were no games scheduled that day.

Darius nodded. "Some kind of epic livestreamed event. Look."

They all crowded around Darius's phone. On the screen they saw silhouettes of LeBron and the Tunes, ready to play basketball.

"In a world inundated with mundanity, one event threatens to blow your mind," Al G.'s voice announced. "In the real world, he's the greatest basketball player who ever lived. The chosen one himself, King James. But here in the Serververse, there's only one man worthy enough to challenge him for the throne."

A silhouette of Dom appeared on the phone's screen.

"His son Dom. It's father versus son in the biggest game in the history of the universe. Welcome to the Space Jam! Only on Warner 3000."

The screen went blank. The family and Malik just stood there for a moment, stunned.

“How can Dad be playing Dom?” asked Xosha, Dom’s little sister.

“More important,” Malik said, “how can the game be playing on Warner 3000? We haven’t even signed a contract!” He thought of something. “If Bron’s tweeting from his phone right now, that means—”

“I can track him on my phone,” Kamiyah said, pulling out her own phone.

“That’s what I was gonna say,” Malik said.

LeBron gathered the Tunes on Lola’s old basketball court. At the whiteboard, he diagrammed his signature move. “Okay,” he said. “One more time. In and out, crossover, step back, shoot.”

“Oooh, that’s some fancy footwork, doc,” Bugs said admiringly. “Let me try.” But when Bugs did the basketball move, it immediately turned into a goofy dance, complete with hilarious foot-pounding, rhythmic music.

"Okay, STOP!" LeBron shouted over the music. "Bugs, I expect more out of you. You already got what you wanted—all your friends back on Tune World. But I still need my son back!" LeBron circled the drawing of the court on the whiteboard with his finger. "Outside these lines, be as looney as you want. But *inside,* you do what I say!"

"Oh, I see," Bugs said, offended. "You're *that* kind of king."

"Look, Bugs," LeBron said firmly. "It's either my way or the highway."

While they were arguing, Lola noticed that the big clock had run almost all the way down, with just a few seconds remaining. She also noticed a rip forming in a wall of the basketball court.

"Uh, guys?" Lola said, trying to get their attention.

"Oh, yeah?" Bugs said, nose to nose with LeBron.

"Yeah," LeBron insisted. "Fundamentals win championships."

CRRRRAAAACK . . .

Bugs and LeBron finally noticed the break in the wall.

"Uh-oh," Bugs said.

“He’s here,” LeBron said, realizing. They looked up and saw Al G.’s gleaming basketball court forming in the air over Lola’s old court.

“GO! GO!” LeBron shouted, pushing everyone off the court. “GET OUT OF THE WAY! GO!”

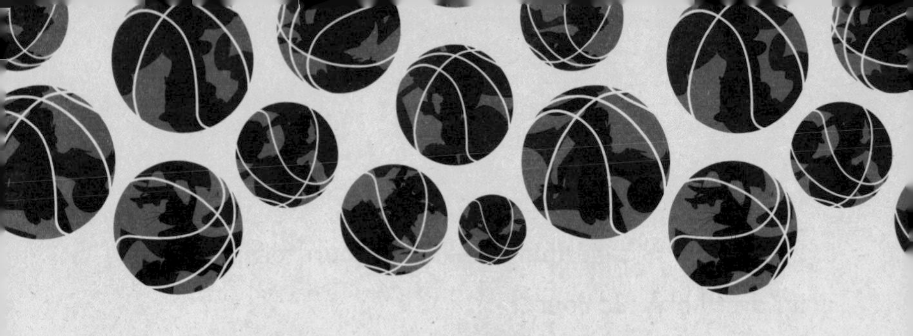

CHAPTER SEVENTEEN

WHAAAAAMMMMM!

Al G.'s Space Jam basketball court slammed down onto the old Looney Tunes court, destroying it! Luckily, the Tunes all managed to dive out of the way before they got squished.

The gleaming, high-tech court went dark. Smoke filled the arena. And then Al G. dropped out of the sky, accompanied by Pete.

"Well, if it isn't the Old News Looney Tunes," the villainous algorithm said. "Looking just as washed-up as ever. I think it's time for an upgrade." He conjured up a digital screen with all the Looney Tunes pictured on it.

"An upgrade?" Bugs asked, puzzled.

Starting with Lola, Al G. turned the Looney Tunes from two-dimensional, flat cartoons into three-dimensional figures.

"What in the world?" Lola said, holding her newly three-dimensional hand in front of her face.

Laughing, Al G. moved onto Foghorn Leghorn.

"I say, I say, cock-a-doodle-do-not-do-that!" the rooster cried as he transformed.

"I look amazing!" Daffy said, admiring his new self.

"What's happening?" LeBron asked just as Al G. turned him from cartoon form back into his normal body. Next to him, Bugs popped into 3-D.

"Oh, no!" he gasped.

The Tunes gathered around LeBron. Al G. admired the digital transformations he'd made. "Lookin' sharp, Looney Tunes!"

Glaring at Al G., LeBron stepped forward. "Where's my son?"

"Oh, *now* you want to be Daddy of the Year?" Al G. taunted. "Just calm down, LeBron. He'll be here. But first, let's get some fans in these seats!"

Al G. and Pete disappeared. Suddenly, the ground began to shake.

On the Warner Bros. lot, Kamiyah tracked her husband's phone. She, Xosha, Darius, and Malik followed the signal to the room full of servers.

"It says he's in here," Kamiyah said, looking around. She saw nothing but computers.

"Yo, Bron!" Malik called. But there was no answer. Only the whir of the fans cooling the computer drives.

SHWOOM! Half of the seats in the huge arena filled up with characters from Warner Bros. movies and TV shows, including King Kong and lots of DC Super Heroes.

Elmer looked up at the empty side of the auditorium. "Where's the other half of the crowd?" he asked.

Al G. reappeared. "I'm glad you asked!" Raising his arms, he sent his computer power crackling out of the Serververse into the outside world. All over the planet, fans tuning in to watch LeBron play were sucked into their phones! They found themselves sitting in the gigantic amphitheater.

Foghorn marveled at all the fans. "I say, I say, how in the world did he get all these spectators here?"

"I don't know," Daffy said. "But the line for the bathroom's gonna be insane. I should go now. Excuse me. . . ."

In the announcers' booth, a sportscaster named Ernie Johnson and a comedian named Lil Rel materialized.

"What are we doing here?" Lil Rel asked, bewildered.

"Looks like we're in some kind of computer-generated basketball game," Ernie said, stating the obvious.

"Look at the size of this crowd!" Al G. exclaimed. "But I think we still have room for a few more courtside. . . ."

Back in the room full of computers, Darius looked at his phone. "Looks like Dad's game is starting."

"What?" Malik said. "Let me see that!"

They gathered around Darius's phone. They saw a gigantic basketball arena, full of spectators except for three empty seats right by the court.

"Got some VIPs comin' in!" Al G. announced.

Then they saw LeBron. "There's Dad!" Darius said.

"This isn't right," Malik said, shaking his head. "We shouldn't be watching this." He walked away from the others.

"Where is he?" Kamiyah asked. "Where's this coming from?"

FLASH! Darius's phone and the servers all lit up at the same time! When Malik turned back, looking for Kamiyah, Darius, and Xosha, they were gone! All that was left was Darius's phone on the floor. Malik ran to pick it up. The screen read WARNER SEATS REDEEMED. ENJOY THE GAME.

"NO!" Malik screamed.

CHAPTER EIGHTEEN

Kamiyah, Darius, and Xosha found themselves sitting courtside in an enormous basketball arena open to the night sky.

Kamiyah gasped. “Whoa. What in the world?”

“Mommy?” Xosha said, scared. “What just happened?”

LeBron spotted his family in the seats. “Kamiyah! Kids!”

“Bron!” Kamiyah called to her husband.

He rushed over to them, but when he tried to hug his wife . . . *BANG!* He hit an invisible force field put in place by Al G. to stop LeBron and the Tunes from interacting with the fans.

“What is going on?” she asked.

“I have to go play this game to save everyone with—”

Bugs popped up over LeBron’s shoulder.

“Bugs Bunny?” Darius said, astonished. “You’re going to play basketball with Bugs Bunny?”

"Eh, what's up, doc?" Bugs said, reaching to shake Darius' hand. *ZWHAM!* The force field sent Bugs flying across the court.

"Yeah, I'm playing with Bugs Bunny," LeBron said, nodding. "That's kinda normal around here."

Darius realized where they were. "Dad," he said, "this is Dom's game. You know how to play, right?"

LeBron looked uncertain. "Of course . . . yeah . . ."

Al G.'s amplified voice interrupted their conversation. "Excuse me! Paging LeBron James!"

"Everything's going to be all right," LeBron assured his family. "I promise." He ran back to his teammates, leaving his wife in shock.

In the room full of computer servers, Malik was yelling into his phone. "Zap me into you! Zap me, the human, into you, the phone! ZAP ME!"

But nothing happened. Malik shook his phone in frustration. Where had everyone gone?

An announcer's voice came over the loudspeaker. "Ladies and gentlemen, please give a warm welcome to your host for the evening, Mr. Al G. Rhythm!"

A spotlight hit Al G. at center court. "Hey, how y'all doin'?" he asked in a friendly voice. The crowd cheered. "Feel the energy in this room! I feel so . . . ALIVE! Oh, man! Dom was right. There really is nothing like a live audience. Thank you! Thank you very much! Ladies and gentlemen, boys and girls, welcome to the first and final Serververse Classic!"

The spectators applauded. They weren't sure what a Serververse Classic was, or who this dude in the shiny getup was, but they knew they were here to see LeBron James play basketball. And to them, that was all that mattered.

"Let me tell you what," Al G. continued, "I know that you are LeBron's biggest fans and the King has had a great run. But that's over. It's time for a new king to take the throne."

"This dude is a hater," LeBron told his teammates by their bench.

"Haters gonna hate," Granny agreed.

"He's a bad guy!" Elmer said, frowning.

"Big-time," LeBron said.

But Al G. wasn't done with his announcements. "Let's lay down some basic ground rules. If King James wins, you all get to go back to your regular, boring lives. But if *my* team wins, you get to stay with me in the Serververse FOREVER!"

The stricken crowd started to boo.

"Wait, what?" LeBron said. "That wasn't the deal!"

"Oh, and I almost forgot," Al G. added. "All of the Tunes will be deleted."

The Tunes were stunned at this news. But before they could react, Al G. went on to introduce his team. The lights dimmed.

"And now," Al G. said dramatically, "from the beautiful mind of Dominic James . . ."

"From the mind of Dominic James?" Kamiyah repeated, still confused about where they were and what was going on.

". . . introducing . . . the GOON SQUAD!" Al G. shouted, opening his arms wide.

Pounding music played and spotlights swung around the court as the players ran out and demonstrated their moves. White Mamba was the snakelike beast Dom had changed Diana Taurasi into. Wet/Fire was a mutated version of Klay Thompson, the player famous for making a splash—a shot that drained right through the net—and being on fire when it came to scoring three-point shots. Wet/Fire combined a wave of water with burning flames. Arachnneka was the result of Dom combining Nneka Ogwumike with a spider (an arachnid) to create a six-armed, web-shooting basketball player. And the Brow was a flying version of Anthony Davis, who was famous for his thick eyebrow.

"Dang!" LeBron said. "What did they do to the Brow?"

Al G. had one more Goon Squad player to introduce. "And this next young man I'm bringing up— Oh, my goodness, y'all gonna love him. He puts the 'G' in 'genius'! He's my hero of the ones and zeroes . . . MR. DOMINIC JAMES!"

Flying in on a wire, Dom was lowered from the ceiling. Waving shyly, he looked excited. The Tunes were shocked to see LeBron's son playing for the opposing team. So was Kamiyah.

"DOM!" she called.

"I don't think he can hear you," Darius said.

"I'm his mother. He *better* hear me! DOM!"

But Darius was right. Dom couldn't hear her. He stared up at the huge crowd of spectators, awed. "Whoa."

"Right?" Al G. said, smiling. "Amazing. All these people came here to see you!"

As Dom tried to take in the size of the audience, his dad ran up to him. "Dom."

"Dad," Dom said.

"Are you okay, son?"

"I've never been better!"

"Listen to me," his father urged. "Everyone here is in danger."

Dom rolled his eyes. "Ugh. Come on, Dad. Why do you have to make everything so serious?"

"This *is* serious," LeBron insisted. "Your boy Al G.—he's a bad dude."

"What?" Dom asked, scrunching up his face in disbelief.

"He's using your game to trap everyone in here," LeBron explained.

But Dom wasn't buying it. "He's not bad. He's just sad because he works so hard and no one pays attention to him. Like me, Dad."

Now it was LeBron's turn to not buy it. "No. He's nothing like you. He's manipulating you!"

Al G. stepped in to interrupt. "Whoa, whoa, whoa," he said to LeBron, holding up both hands. "Why are you using all these charged words? 'Trap.' 'Manipulate.'" He put his hands over Dom's ears and whispered, "Kidnapped." Removing his hands from Dom's ears, Al G. said, "Come on, LeBron. Chill out."

But LeBron was far from chilled out. He was focused on Al G. saying 'Kidnapped.' "What did you say, man?" he demanded.

Dom faced his dad. "I'm playing basketball. I thought you'd be happy."

"'Thought you'd be happy,'" Al G. echoed, shaking his head sadly. "LeBron, you keep it up, you ain't gonna get that Father's Day card. Those things are not guaranteed."

LeBron ignored him, still trying to get his son to listen to his warnings. "Dom!"

The four monstrous members of the Goon Squad stepped in, ending the conversation. The Brow stared down at LeBron. "You're going down, King James," he growled.

LeBron turned and walked toward his wife. The Brow looked offended.

"We'll show him who's boss," White Mamba hissed.

As LeBron approached, Kamiyah asked anxiously, "What'd Dom say, Bron?"

LeBron looked disappointed. "He thinks Al G. is his friend. I don't know what to do."

"You've got to win this game and get our son back," she said firmly.

Taking a deep breath and letting it out, LeBron nodded and said, determined, "I will."

CHAPTER NINETEEN

"It's game time!" said the announcer. The crowd cheered as the starting lineups for each team took their places around center court. The Tune Squad started with LeBron, Bugs, Lola, Sylvester, and Tweety. They were facing off against Dom, Wet/Fire, White Mamba, Arachnneka, and the Brow. LeBron and Dom would jump for the tip-off.

Bugs gave LeBron a fist bump. The ref stepped into the circle with the ball. LeBron recognized the little robot.

"Pete's the referee?" LeBron asked. He seriously doubted Al G.'s personal assistant would call the game fairly. This was going to be tough.

TWEEEEEET! Pete blew his whistle to start the game. In the announcers' booth, Ernie Johnson said, "Look, I don't want to alarm you or any of our viewers, but apparently if the Tune Squad doesn't win this game, we're all going to be trapped in here forever."

Laughing, Lil Rel said, "Luckily the Tune Squad's got the four-time MVP LeBron James on their team. I ain't sweatin' it."

Dom stepped on a power-up and rose high above the floor. Pete tossed the ball *way* up in the air.

LeBron watched, shocked, as Dom controlled the tip. "You gotta be kidding me!" he said.

"Oh, we're doomed! WE'RE DOOMED!" Lil Rel cried, instantly reversing himself. "Did you see that kid fly?"

"Uh-huh," Ernie said.

"He's like Superman but with a high-top fade!" Lil Rel observed.

Dom slammed the ball down to Wet/Fire, who splashed across the court and passed to Arachnneka. She tossed the ball up near the basket. White Mamba sprang into the air and whipped the ball down through the hoop for a windmill dunk! The game gave the Goon Squad bonus points for scoring first, and for doing it with incredible showmanship.

"What's with the score?" LeBron asked, bewildered. By his count, the Goons should have only scored two.

"It's style points, Dad," Dom explained.

"Style points?" LeBron said. In the game he knew and loved, there were no style points.

In the announcers' booth, Ernie was puzzled, too. "Style points?"

"We're playing video game rules! You get extra points for scoring with style!" Lil Rel explained. "Style points, power-ups . . . See, kids? Playing video games *does* pay off!"

The Tunes tried to bring the ball downcourt, but Arachnneka stole it with her sticky web! She went straight to the basket, scoring over and over with her six arms.

"Is this legal?" Ernie asked Lil Rel.

"Yeah," Lil Rel said. "She's got six arms. What else is she supposed to do?"

Bugs ran up to LeBron, who couldn't believe the stuff the ref was allowing.

"Listen, Bron-Bron," Bugs said. "This is basketball, but with a spin to it! We gotta think outta the box!"

"There's only one basketball," LeBron insisted. "And, Bugs—don't do anything looney. Let's go!"

"Nothing looney?" Bugs said. "We're not called the Fundamental Tunes!"

From the bench, Daffy yelled, "Don't just stand there, rabbit! Get the ball to LeBron!" Bugs passed to LeBron, who took the ball downcourt and faced off against his son.

"LeBron's so hard to guard down low," Ernie pointed out, "using that great size advantage."

Towering over Dom, LeBron said, "Sorry, son. You know I got to win this game. It's for your own good."

"If you say so," Dom replied. LeBron took his shot, but Dom jumped on a power-up, zoomed into the air, and snatched the ball, still on its way up, before it reached the basket. A clean block!

A couple plays later, Dom stole the ball and bounced it between LeBron's legs. But the ball came down from the high bounce just short of the basket. At the last second, Pete flew in and moved the basket. The Goons scored!

"Oh, yes!" Al G. cheered. "See, this is why we practice!" He looked around and admitted, "We didn't. We don't practice."

CHAPTER TWENTY

LeBron couldn't believe the ref had just moved the basket so the other team could score! "What's up with that, Pete?" he demanded.

Pete tried to argue, but LeBron cut him off. "Oh, you didn't hear what I said? You heard exactly what I said. You can't move the basket like that! Man, that's cheating!"

"No, you can," Al G. disagreed. "You can move the basket."

"You don't even know what you're talking about," LeBron said. He noticed Pete starting to make a T shape with his hands. "Oh, a technical foul? You're gonna give me a technical? Man, I wish you would!" Dismissing Pete with a wave of his arm, LeBron stormed away from him.

But from the bench, Foghorn was still complaining to Pete. "I say, what kind of ship are you running here?

You got to call the game fair, I say, FAIR!" *TWEEEET!* Pete blew his whistle and threw Foghorn out of the game!

"Never in my career did I think I'd say these five words," Ernie said in the booth. "Foghorn Leghorn just got ejected!"

LeBron kept scoring, but so did the Goons. With style points, the Goon Squad was way up. Bugs called for a time-out.

At the Tunes' bench, LeBron spoke to his teammates. "All right, what are we doing? Good, clean, fundamental basketball. Keep the ball moving from side to side. We gotta keep playing for one another and keep the energy going. We're right there."

Fed up with another of LeBron's typical lectures, Bugs jumped up, grabbed him, and shook him. "This isn't regular basketball! When are you gonna get that through your thick skull, Mr. Fundamental?"

Elmer pulled Bugs off LeBron. "Hey, stay off him!"

"Why, you—" Bugs said to Elmer. They started fighting, somehow raising a cloud of dust off the shiny, polished floor.

LeBron tried to break up the fight. "Elmer, take it easy!"

Sylvester shoved Elmer. "Watch yourself, buster!"

"You monsta!" Tweety shouted at Sylvester accusingly. The cat responded by grabbing the little bird and stuffing him in his mouth.

"Hey!" LeBron scolded Sylvester. "You get Tweety out of your mouth!"

"Ya varmint!" Yosemite Sam yelled at Sylvester as he shook the cat, making him spit Tweety out.

"Yosemite, chill!" LeBron said, trying to calm his teammates down.

Taz started spinning like a tornado, knocking players right and left. "RARRR-SWARRRRRZZZ-AAARRR!"

"TAZ! STOP!" LeBron barked, trying to grab the whirling animal. "You guys are worse than my kids!"

Seeing the chaos erupting around the Tunes' bench, Al G. grinned and said, "Perfect. They're fighting amongst themselves. Falling apart. It's exactly what we want. But I guess it's time to put them out of their misery." He turned to Dom. "Go ahead and take a little break, Dom. Because you know what time it is?"

"What time is it, Al?" Dom asked, smiling.

"Oh, it's Dame Time," Al G. said.

DAME TIME appeared on the scoreboard in bright red letters. The announcer said over the speaker system, "New character unlocked!"

"New character?" LeBron said, looking up at the scoreboard.

"Well, here's our first Goon Squad substitution of the night," Ernie Johnson said. "Let's see who it is. . . ."

"CHROOONOOOS!" called the announcer, drawing out the name.

The character that Dom had created with his scan of Damian Lillard zipped onto the court, moving so quickly, he looked blurred. Because Damian had suggested the Dame Time playing mode, Dom had provided his avatar with a watch that gave him special powers.

"I'm the king stopper!" Chronos boasted, pointing at LeBron.

Seeing how fast this new player was, Daffy decided to make a couple of changes of his own. "Granny, I'm subbing you out. Speedy, Road Runner—you're in."

"Beep! Beep!" said Road Runner, heading onto the court.

Speedy threw the ball to Lola. As she dribbled and started moving downcourt, Al G. handed Dom a tub of popcorn. Laughing, Al said, "Knock yourself out, kid. This should be good."

"CHROOOONOOOOS!" howled a fan in the audience.

Chronos tapped his watch . . . and everything went into slow motion.

Everything except Chronos, who kept right on moving and scoring at full speed!

CHAPTER TWENTY-ONE

BRRZZZZT!

As the buzzer went off, calling halftime, Bugs listened to the cheers for the other team and felt defeated. So did Lola, Daffy, and the other Tunes. Chronos had racked up a ton of points for the Goon Squad. How could they possibly come back from such a big deficit?

In the locker room, Lola tried to rally her teammates. "Come on, guys! There's a whole other half to play. We can still win this!"

The others sat on benches or leaned against lockers, moping. "How?" Porky asked. "We're getting decimated."

"Porky's right," Bugs said. "We're sinking faster than the *Titanic*."

Daffy paced back and forth, thinking. "We need a boost. A pick-me-up. A secret weapon."

"We need a miracle," Granny said.

"We can't give up hope yet," Lola insisted. "They're called comebacks for a reason."

Even LeBron thought Lola was being unrealistic. "We're down a thousand points! No team comes back from that!"

Drawing himself up to his full height (which still barely reached LeBron's waist), Yosemite Sam snarled, "Well, why don't you try coaching us better, bucko?"

LeBron couldn't believe his ears. "I've been trying to save my son and coach you all at the same time. What're *y'all* doing?"

Lola stepped forward. "We've been trying!"

"Trying to do what?" LeBron asked.

"Trying to be like you," Lola said.

LeBron went silent. He looked at the discouraged faces of the Tunes staring back at him.

"And it's not working," Bugs said.

"Because you're not me," LeBron said, realizing. He looked down at his shoes and remembered what his son had said to him: "You never let me just do me." He made a decision.

Grabbing a marker, LeBron crossed over to a whiteboard. "Okay, I got it. New game plan. Bugs, time to do what you guys do best." He handed the marker to Bugs. The bunny's face lit up as he took it.

"You know something?" he said. "If we're going out, we're going out looney."

Lola smiled a big smile.

"Now, here's what we're going to do . . . ," Bugs said, starting to draw on the board.

Al G. waited impatiently for the Tune Squad to come out and play the second half of the game. He was enjoying their humiliation, and planned to have his Goons run up the score as high as possible.

WHOOOOSH! The ramp lowered from Marvin the Martian's spaceship. Daffy came out and quickly set up a banner with the Looney Tunes logo on it. He hurried back up the ramp, and then ran down with Porky. They burst through the banner.

"It's showtime!" Daffy announced.

The other members of the Tune Squad followed them through the hole in the banner, ready for the second half! LeBron high-fived his teammates. "Yeah, let's go, Tunes! Are we ready? Tune Squad in the house! Let's go!"

LeBron glared at Al G. Then he and his teammates made big goofy faces at the algorithm. LeBron's family laughed. That was their dad, having fun!

Al G. looked annoyed. Next to him, Dom couldn't help smiling.

In the announcers' booth, Ernie Johnson said, "They may be down a gazillion points, but LeBron James and the Tunes are coming back out here for the third quarter with some renewed energy."

"And I don't understand why," Lil Rel said. "They are losing really badly."

BRRRRRT! The buzzer sounded, signaling the start of the second half.

It was now or never. . . .

CHAPTER TWENTY-TWO

Tweety had the ball. He looked up and saw the Brow looming over him. "Uh-oh," Tweety said. "Do you have your ticket?"

"Ticket?" the Brow asked, confused. "What ticket?"

WHAM! A train roared out of a tunnel painted on the wall by Wile E. Coyote, knocking the Brow clean out of the way!

"Your train ticket! Classic!" Tweety said, passing the ball to Bugs. Wet/Fire charged toward Bugs, but Gossamer got in between, using his furry body to absorb the splashy player like a big red sponge. *SHHHHLLORP!*

"*Someone's* absorbed in the game!" Bugs wisecracked, firing a quick pass to LeBron, who whistled for Road Runner. The bird took the ball and was long gone by the time the Goon Squad surrounded LeBron.

"Hey, guys," LeBron said to them in a friendly voice. They turned and took off after Road Runner, who'd kicked up a thick dust cloud.

What they didn't realize was that Road Runner had dished the ball off to Tweety under the cover of that dust cloud.

WHAM! Tweety jammed the ball through the hoop, giving a triumphant yell. "AAAAHHHH!" Not only did he score the basket, but Tweety's team received a smokescreen bonus.

Al G. couldn't believe it. "Oh, no! Are you kidding me? A Road Runner smokescreen? It's the oldest trick in the book!"

"TWEETY!" LeBron cheered.

"Woo-hoo!" Lola whooped. "Yes! We got this!"

Grabbing a big microphone, Bugs took over the play-by-play description of the game. "Dom passes to Wet/Fire. Wet/Fire back to Brow. He's going to dunk, but . . . he freezes!"

Sure enough, the Brow found himself frozen over the rim, unable to slam the ball home. He had no idea what was happening. Dom was puzzled, too. He didn't know a player could control his game just by announcing what was happening through an old-fashioned microphone.

"And now the Brow builds an enormous bird's nest," Bugs continued. Controlled by Bugs's words, the Brow made a nest on top of the basket, settled into it, and squawked like a crow. *"CAW! CAW!"*

Al G. jumped to his feet and yelled at the Brow. "What are you *doin'?*"

"Oooh, looks like he's really rufflin' some feathers!" Bugs said, seeing how mad the bird-Brow was making Al G.

The algorithm stormed over to Bugs, snatched the microphone out of his hands, and tossed it aside. The Brow, looking a little embarrassed, destroyed the nest and jumped down from the basket. He took off running after Taz, who was heading toward the other basket with the ball, speaking his own language.

"BLARGA-BLARG-BLAGA-BLAH!"

When the Brow caught up with Taz, he stole the ball and knocked him down. LeBron helped Taz up. Then he made a spinning motion with his hand and said, "Taz, blarga-blarg-blaga-blah!" Taz nodded and grinned, showing his fangs. He started spinning, turning faster and faster until he drilled down into the hardwood floor of the basketball court and spun the whole court around 180 degrees!

SLAM! The Brow made a tremendous dunk . . . IN THE TUNE SQUAD'S BASKET! The Tune Squad got the points for the basket AND a bonus for "full-court twist." The crowd—especially LeBron's family—cheered!

"Are you serious?" Al G. ranted.

"YEAH!" LeBron said, congratulating Taz. "Blarga-blarg-blaga-BLAH!"

Furious, Al G. yelled at the referee. "Make a call, Pete! Don't tell me you're neutral!"

Dom saw Al G. yelling at Pete, and he didn't like it. . . .

Dom's mom stood up and started a chant. "LET'S GO, TUNES! LET'S GO, TUNES!" Soon the whole crowd had taken up the chant. "LET'S GO, TUNES! LET'S GO, TUNES!"

"Wow!" Ernie said in the booth. "Check out this crowd. Everyone's really getting behind the Tune Squad."

"You know something?" Lil Rel said, "It's about time."

Al G. sat on the Goon Squad bench nervously chewing on a towel. Pete flew in next to him with a big grin on his face. Al G. turned and glared at his assistant. Pete dropped his smile.

Out on the court, Wile E. Coyote poured a box of birdseed onto a ball launcher's button. He whistled for Road Runner, who zipped up and started pecking at the pile of seeds. *PECK! PECK! PECK! PECK! PECK!*

Every time Road Runner hit the button, another basketball flew out of the launcher. Wile E. opened up an Acme Multiplying Machine to catch the balls. Then the multiplier shot *hundreds* of basketballs toward the Tunes Squad's basket! Wile E. was making it rain!

"Whoa!" Dom said, watching all the balls head toward the basket.

Though he scored tons of points, Wile E. also got hit in the face by dozens of balls. He held up a sign that read OUCH.

Dom and the crowd laughed. Al G. glared at Dom.

"What's wrong, Al?" Dom asked. "That was awesome."

"What do you mean, what's wrong?" Al G. raged. "They're catching up!" He whispered into his headset microphone, "Run Dame Time."

CHAPTER TWENTY-THREE

Like a flash, Chronos sped onto the court.

"Not him again!" LeBron said by the Tunes' bench.

Granny hopped off the bench. "I got this whippersnapper," she said, grabbing her walker.

"Are you sure about this, Granny?" LeBron asked as she slowly moved across the court, one step at a time.

"I'm going old-school on him," she answered.

Rapidly bouncing the ball, Chronos watched as Granny did a ninja move over her walker, landing in a martial arts pose.

"Whoa," LeBron said, amazed at the old lady's agility.

Without breaking her pose, Granny held out a cupped hand and moved her fingers, making a "come here" gesture to Chronos. Curious, he started to dribble the ball toward her. When he'd crossed half the distance, Granny yelled, "STOP!"

As Chronos slowed down, Granny vaulted over him, reaching down to turn up the dial on his watch. This sped up his life time, causing Chronos to age decades in seconds! Before she landed, Granny kicked the basketball through the basket, scoring extra points for her "senior discount"!

Furious, Al G. shouted, "What is going on out there?"

The Tunes were rapidly catching up. Lola brought the ball down the court on a fast break, jumping over Arachnneka and sliding under the Brow.

"Lola!" LeBron called, signaling for her to throw the ball high. She launched it, and LeBron jumped on a power-up, sending himself high enough to catch the ball and slam it through the hoop. He scored half-court dunk points, and the crowd went wild!

"The Tunes take the lead with a monster slam!" Ernie announced. "Oh, what a play for Lola and LeBron James! Can the Tunes hold on to this lead?"

"I'll tell you this," Lil Rel said. "I woke up today and only knew one world. Then I got sucked into my phone! At this point, *anything* is possible."

LeBron ran over to the Tunes' bench and celebrated with his teammates. Then he turned to the arena and waved his arms, rallying the crowd. "This is fun basketball right here!" he said. "Be yourselves! Be yourselves!"

Dom watched his dad, wanting to be with him.

Al G. noticed. "Hey, Dom—are you a Tune? Or a Goon? Tune or Goon? Make up your mind!" Dom sat on the Goon bench.

LeBron was still celebrating. "Yeah! Way to get looney out there!" He shot a glance at Al G., knowing the crowd's reaction and the Tunes' joy were getting to him.

In the break before the final quarter, Al G. addressed his team, smiling his friendliest smile. "Everybody happy, huh? Everybody having a good time? Yeah, you having a lot of fun out there? 'Cause that's all that matters, right? That you're having fun?" In an instant, he switched from fake friendly to genuinely angry. "THAT DOESN'T MATTER AT ALL! WHAT MATTERS IS THAT I WIN THIS GAME!"

He spun to face Dom directly. "Oh, and *you,* Dom! How are you losing at *your own game*? I didn't even think that was possible. I expected a lot more out of you, son. Get your head in the game. I *need* to win."

Dom didn't enjoy being yelled at. He looked over at the Tunes' bench. LeBron noticed.

Al G. was still ranting. "Yeah, maybe your dad was right about you. Letting you be you was a mistake."

Seeing Al G. yell at his son made LeBron furious.

"LeBron," Lola said, watching him fume. "Hey, are you with us?"

"Let's end this," LeBron said. "I'm getting my son back." He and the Tunes marched onto the court.

Lola inbounded the ball to LeBron, who motioned for his teammates to move to one side of the floor.

"Iso!" he said, calling for an isolation play, one-on-one. "Clear out!" He squared off against Dom, dribbling, ready to make his move.

"I wonder what move he's gonna do," Lola said.

"The post-up?" Sylvester guessed.

"Maybe the fadeaway," Yosemite Sam suggested.

Daffy shook his head. "He's gonna dunk all over him. Look at that kid! Kid's too small!"

LeBron leaned over and put one shoulder down as though he was about to charge straight through Dom to the basket . . .

. . . but then he stopped.

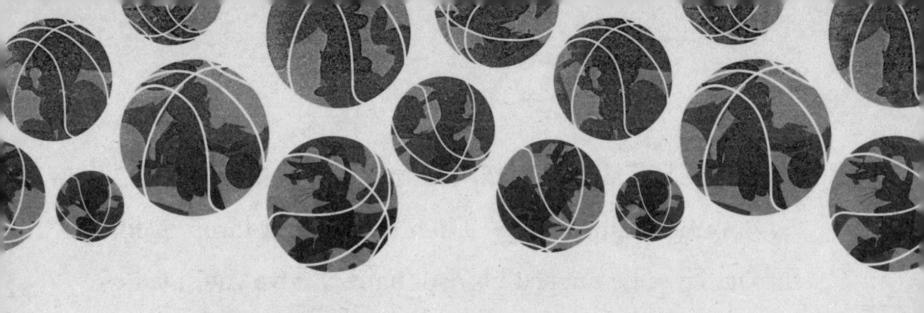

CHAPTER TWENTY-FOUR

Dom was confused. "Dad, what are you doing? We're in the middle of a game."

LeBron smiled. "Dom, this game of yours is *amazing.* I guess I would've known that if I'd listened more. Sorry I didn't."

He paused, wanting to get the words just right. "For me, when I was a kid, the things that I went through to get where I am now, I had to be a certain way. It helped me win games, but not so much with being a dad."

Dom looked close to tears. He couldn't believe his dad was telling him this.

"I'm still learning how to be a dad," LeBron said. "You're teaching me. I want you to be yourself. Do you understand how much I love you? Do you understand how important you are to me? How overwhelming that is? I mean, I don't even know if I'm saying this right." He tossed the ball away, getting frustrated with himself.

"Sounds right to me," Dom said with a lump in his throat. Then he hugged his dad, hard. "I love you, Dad."

"I love you, too, son."

The crowd applauded! On the Tunes' bench, LeBron's teammates were amazed and impressed by what he'd done.

"Hey, all right!" Yosemite Sam whooped. "Way to go! Woooo!"

"I think I'm gonna cry," Lola said.

Daffy was already sobbing and blowing his nose loudly. *HONK!*

But Al G. didn't find this touching moment between a father and his son the least bit moving. "Are you serious?" he called to Dom. "You two are a joke! You know that?"

LeBron started to storm over to Al G., but Dom stopped him. "I got this, Dad." He walked over to the Goons' bench.

"You got something to say?" Al G. asked.

"Yeah," Dom said calmly and confidently. "I think you want people to fear you more than anything, and I'm not about that, Al G. I'm playing with my dad."

"First of all," Al G. said, seething with anger, "it's Mr. Rhythm to you, you little traitor. Second of all, you're not. You're playing *against* your dad." He pointed to Dom's jersey. "See what that says? Goon Squad. You already made your choice, Dom."

Pete swooped down in his ref's shirt. Al G. turned to him. "Right, Pete? He can't—" Al G. noticed Pete wiping away a tear. "Pete, are you crying? There's no crying in the Serververse, Pete!"

Pete flew away, and Dom walked over to the Tunes' bench.

"Ohhhh, all right," Al G. said. "Yeah, all right. I see how it is, Dom. I see how it is! I GAVE YOU EVERYTHING!"

Thrilled with Dom's arrival, the Tunes welcomed him to their team.

"I made this just in case," Granny said, passing LeBron an extra Tune Squad jersey.

"Thanks, Granny," LeBron said. He handed the jersey to his son.

"Here you go, Dom."

"Thanks, Dad."

Dom pulled the jersey over his head. He was ready to play as a Tune!

Al G. was standing at center court. "Fine," he said. "You wanna join these losers? You go ahead, Dom. 'Cause it's not your game anymore. I *am* the game!"

Al G.'s fingers started to glow green. He lifted them, morphing himself taller, bigger, stronger—even bigger and stronger than LeBron! The Goons gathered behind him and he shot his energy into them, making them even bigger than they already were! Huge! Gigantic! Massive!

Daffy gulped.

"Yo, King!" Al G. roared, taunting LeBron. "You're about to lose your family, your friends, those Tunes—everything you love!"

LeBron's eyes narrowed, full of resolve. "I don't think so."

"Oh, it's on," Bugs said. He and LeBron bumped fists.

Now that they had Dom on their team, the Tunes were determined to win. They ran out onto the court, clashing with the Goons! Al G. used his teammates as a ladder to climb up and dunk right over LeBron!

"I'm a monster!" Al G. bragged. "It's over!"

But it wasn't over quite yet. With seconds left to play, the Tunes were down by just one point. LeBron called a time-out.

The Tune Squad huddled up by their bench.

"All we gotta do is get one bucket," LeBron said.

Daffy glanced at their opponents. "Yeah, but there's an awful lot of Goon Squad between us and that bucket."

"Listen," LeBron said. "Just get me the ball. Hands in." They stacked their hands in the center of their circle. "Tune Squad on three. One, two, three . . ."

"TUNE SQUAD!" they all yelled.

Lola fired the ball to LeBron. He raced down the court toward the basket with all the Goons in hot pursuit. Spotting a power-up, LeBron leapt for it and rose into the air! He raised the ball above his head, ready to slam it down for the game-winning dunk . . .

. . . but Al G. was right in front of him, pushing him back!

"He's not gonna make it!" Bugs cried. "He's not—"

"—gonna make it," Lola said.

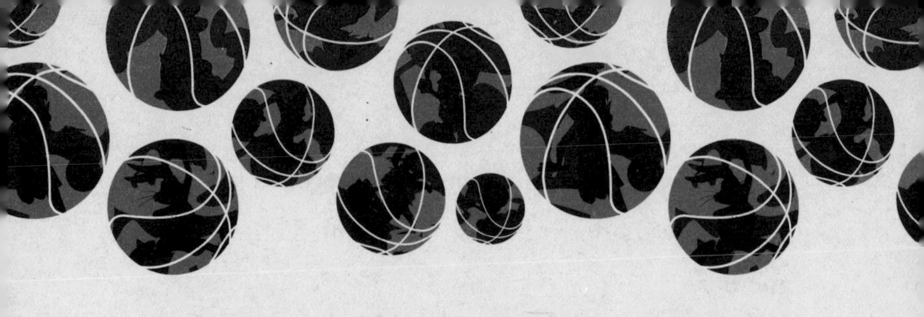

CHAPTER TWENTY-FIVE

Al G. grinned in evil triumph.

"He's blocking my shot!" LeBron thought. Then . . .

Dom grabbed a power-up disk and threw it toward his dad. The disk landed next to LeBron, who jumped on the power-up and soared to the basket. From high in the air, LeBron threw the ball down through the hoop! The buzzer sounded! *BRRRNNNN!*

The game was over, and the Tunes had won! And LeBron's dunk was so amazing, Al G. was turned into an actual poster! In normal basketball, when players got awesomely dunked on, people said they'd been "posterized," because their picture was sure to end up on a poster of the dunk. But in Dom's game, when you got dunked on so massively, you could turn into a real poster! And that's exactly what happened to Al G!

"Posterized!" Dom cheered. "Yeah!!"

"THE TUNES WIN! THE TUNES WIN!" Lil Rel screamed.

"Un-be-liev-able!" Ernie Johnson added. "Al G. just got turned into a literal poster."

Stuck in the poster, Al G. sighed, "This is not how I wanted to go out." Then . . . *SMACK!* Pete burst through the poster, busting it into a million pieces! Al G. was no more.

Daffy ran around the court, looking for someone—anyone—to hug. "Woo-hoo! Woo-hoo! Woo-hoo! We won! We did it! WE WON!"

"WOOOOO!" LeBron whooped. "I love y'all! Yeah, Tunes!"

They all hugged and celebrated, jumping up and down for joy.

Dom ran over to his dad. "All right, Dad!" They hugged as the crowd started to disappear, returning to their homes all over Earth and in the Serververse.

Lola approached LeBron. "Goodbye, Bron," she said. "Thank you for bringing me home."

"Thank you, Lola," LeBron said, "for helping me get my son back."

Waving goodbye, the Tunes shimmered and disappeared, instantly finding themselves back on Looney Tunes World. When they got there, they looked around and saw that their world looked new—shiny, repaired, and ready for all the looniness they could dish out!

"Woo-hoo!" Daffy cheered.

Lola hugged Bugs. "You did it, Bugs!"

"*We* did it," he said. "Welcome home, Lola," he said. "It's great to have you back. Now let's get looney!"

In the computer room at Warner Bros., the servers flashed, then LeBron and his family materialized out of thin air. They all hugged, thrilled to be safely back in the real world together.

"All my family," LeBron said. "Love you guys."

"Love you, too," Kamiyah said.

Malik ran up, thrilled to see his friends. "Bron! You're back!"

"Come on, Malik," LeBron said, holding out a welcoming arm. "Come on in, man."

Malik joined the group hug.

"Let's go home," LeBron said.

A week later, LeBron and Dom walked down the street together. Dom carried a basketball tucked under his arm.

"Dom, you ready for basketball camp?" LeBron asked, smiling.

"Yeah," Dom said, though he was still nervous about going. "I'm actually pretty excited."

Surprised, LeBron said, "Yeah? Because I know how much you wanted—"

"I think I'm gonna just take a break from video games for now," Dom continued. "After we, you know . . ."

"Kinda got sucked into one?"

"Yeah," Dom said, nodding and smiling.

LeBron grinned. "Really?" he asked. "Because I feel like I've made a mistake. We can turn around right now if you want to."

Dom looked puzzled. "What are you talking about?"

"Look," LeBron said, gesturing ahead of them.

Dom looked and saw a sign that said GAME DESIGN CAMP. Not basketball camp! His father had brought him to the game camp instead! Dom's eyes lit up. He couldn't believe it!

LeBron and Dom stopped, looking at the entrance. Then LeBron turned to his son and looked him in the eye. "I figured it's about time for you to do you."

Dom smiled and gave his dad a big hug. "Thank you, Dad."

"You're welcome," LeBron said, pleased to make his son happy. "Hey, man—have fun."

Letting go of his dad, Dom eagerly hurried toward the camp. But LeBron called after him. "Yo, Dom!"

Dom stopped and turned back. LeBron pointed to the basketball still tucked under his son's arm. "The ball."

Dom looked down at it, then back up at his dad. "I think I'll hold on to it," he said.

LeBron smiled. Dom turned and ran into the game camp, and his proud dad watched him go.

Wile E. Coyote

Wile E. Coyote uses Acme gadgets to help the Tune Squad win!

Road Runner

Road Runner is so fast, a cloud of dust appears behind him—the perfect cover for a trick shot!

Gossamer

Gossamer doesn't know his own strength—and he's got the popped basketballs to prove it!

Marvin the Martian

Marvin the Martian is in charge of the team's transportation!

Sylvester & Tweety

Sylvester and Tweety are both light on their feet, making them a great duo—when they aren't on opposing teams!

Porky Pig
What does Porky say at the end of every basketball game? "That's *ball*, folks!"
Yosemite Sam
Sam's favorite move is the Yosemite Slam!

LeBron James
In the Serververse, LeBron leads the Tune Squad!
TUNE SQUAD

Bugs Bunny
Bugs's special shot is called the Hare Ball!
TUNE SQUAD

Daffy Duck
Daffy's favorite play is the Quack Attack!
TUNE SQUAD

Lola Bunny
Lola's special shot is called the Amazonian Alley-Oop!
TUNE SQUAD